"You're supposed to be dead."

Her voice had a raw, uneven tone, the shaking in her hand growing to an alarming wobble as Sin stared down the muzzle of her Glock.

"You didn't blow yourself up," she muttered.

"Says who?" he asked.

"You're wanted by the FBI."

"I'm not on the list anymore," he disagreed. "Dead, you see."

Her mouth twisted with frustration. "You're not dead. And you're under arrest."

He couldn't hold back a grin at her serious expression.

"This isn't funny." Moving more quickly than he thought she could, she grabbed the Glock he'd taken from her and swung it back in front of her. This time, her hands didn't shake nearly as hard.

Fear battled with grudging admiration. She was tougher than she looked. "What are you going to do, shoot me?"

"If I have to."

DEAD MAN'S CURVE

PAULA GRAVES

For Gayle Cochrane, who knows just how many ways I owe her my gratitude. Thanks for all you do!

ISBN-13: 978-0-373-69784-7

DEAD MAN'S CURVE

This edition published by arrangement with Harlequin Books S.A.

For questions and comments about the quality of this book, please contact us at CustomerService@Harlequin.com.

Printed in U.S.A.

ABOUT THE AUTHOR

Alabama native Paula Graves wrote her first book, a mystery starring herself and her neighborhood friends, at the age of six. A voracious reader, Paula loves books that pair tantalizing mystery with compelling romance. When she's not reading or writing, she works as a creative director for a Birmingham advertising agency and spends time with her family and friends. She is a member of Southern Magic Romance Writers, Heart of Dixie Romance Writers and Romance Writers of America.

Paula invites readers to visit her website, www.paulagraves.com.

Books by Paula Graves

HARLEQUIN INTRIGUE

926—FORBIDDEN TERRITORY
998—FORBIDDEN TEMPTATION
1046—FORBIDDEN TOUCH
1088—COWBOY ALIBI
1183—CASE FILE: CANYON CREEK, WYOMING*
1189—CHICKASAW COUNTY CAPTIVE*
1224—ONE TOUGH MARINE*
1230—BACHELOR SHERIFF*
1272—HITCHED AND HUNTED**
1278—THE MAN FROM GOSSAMER RIDGE**
1285—COOPER VENGEANCE**
1305—MAJOR NANNY
1337—SECRET IDENTITY†
1342—SECRET HIDEOUT†
1348—SECRET AGENDA†
1366—SECRET ASSIGNMENT†
1372—SECRET KEEPER†
1378—SECRET INTENTIONS†
1428—MURDER IN THE SMOKIES‡‡
1432—THE SMOKY MOUNTAIN MIST‡‡
1438—SMOKY RIDGE CURSE‡‡
1473—BLOOD ON COPPERHEAD TRAIL‡‡
1479—THE SECRET OF CHEROKEE COVE‡‡
1486—THE LEGEND OF SMUGGLER'S CAVE‡‡
1517—DEAD MAN'S CURVEΔ

*Cooper Justice
**Cooper Justice: Cold Case Investigation
†Cooper Security
‡‡Bitterwood P.D.
ΔThe Gates

CAST OF CHARACTERS

Ava Trent—Assigned to investigate the kidnapping of a married couple, the last thing the up-and-coming FBI agent expects to find is a dead man who's very much alive—and even more dangerous than she remembered.

Sinclair Solano—His time on the FBI's Most Wanted list ended with his presumed death five years earlier. But when his sister's kidnapped, a pawn in an unfinished game of revenge, the former radical must risk coming out of the shadows.

Alexander Quinn—The former CIA agent gave Sinclair the undercover assignment that put him in a terrorist's crosshairs. But without the CIA's resources, can the CEO of The Gates, a high-octane private investigation agency, help his former contact?

Ernesto Cabrera—Having discovered Sinclair's betrayal, the terrorist leader is willing to use the man's sister to draw him into the open.

Alicia Cooper—Sinclair's sister has no idea her brother's alive or why Cabrera has taken her captive.

Gabe Cooper—Alicia's husband, kidnapped with her, has disappeared completely. Did Cabrera order his execution?

Jesse Cooper—Gabe's cousin—and Alicia's boss at Cooper Security—isn't about to stay out of the search for the missing couple.

Cade Landry—Ava's FBI partner is keeping secrets. Could any of them threaten Ava and her investigation?

Chapter One

Special Agent Ava Trent took a slow turn around Room 125 of the Mountain View Motor Lodge, studying everything, even though the Tennessee Bureau of Investigation had already given the place a thorough once-over that morning before the locals had called in the FBI. She doubted there was much they'd missed, but she liked to walk through a crime scene while it was still relatively fresh.

She wasn't going to pretend she could put herself in the head of either the victims or the perpetrator—she'd leave the hocus-pocus to the Investigative Services Unit. She just wanted to get a good look at the setup. Get a picture of it in her head. Most people in law enforcement had their own rituals. Taking a good, long look around a crime scene was hers.

Unmade queen-size bed. Suitcases open, partially unpacked, on the luggage stand helpfully supplied by the Mountain View Motor Lodge. Two toothbrushes in the bathroom.

Blotches of blood on the torn green comforter hanging off the bed.

"Married couple. Gabe and Alicia Cooper." Cade Landry, the agent assigned to investigate the possible kidnapping with her, strode up to her, all broad shoulders, square chin and no nonsense. He was new to the Johnson City, Tennessee, resident agency and, if his gruff demeanor was anything to go by, he wasn't going to turn out to be a favorite among the other agents.

She didn't care herself. She wasn't looking to have her hand held, and if she wanted conversation, she could call up her mother or her sister and get all she could handle. And unlike the female support staff at the resident agency, who all found Landry's rock-hewn features and sweet molasses drawl irresistible, she certainly wasn't in the market for a romantic entanglement, especially not with a fellow agent.

"Plenty of signs of a struggle, but not serious injury," Landry continued. "Blood on the bedspread looks incidental. Bloody nose, maybe. Busted lip in a fight. If the Coopers are deceased, it didn't happen here."

"Why were they here in Poe Creek?" she asked.

"Three-year wedding anniversary, according to the motel staff," Landry answered.

"An anniversary trip to Poe Creek?" She took another look around the motel room and shook her head.

"The husband's a pro fisherman. Seems his idea of an anniversary trip included fishing on Douglas Lake," Landry explained, referring to a lake northeast of Knoxville, Tennessee. It was a fifteen-minute drive from Poe Creek, depending on where they'd planned to put their boat in the water.

"Where can I get me a romantic man like that?" she murmured.

It might have been her imagination, but she thought she spotted a hint of a smile flicker over Landry's stony features. Just a hint, then it was gone. "Not an angler?" he asked as he followed her on her circuit of the room.

"Actually, I'm a very good angler," she answered. "But

I don't reckon scaling fish ranks high on my list of things to do on an anniversary trip." Not that she'd ever had an anniversary to celebrate. Unless you counted six years with the FBI.

"Maybe he does all the fish-cleaning. A woman might find that romantic." Pulling out a pen, Landry nudged a piece of paper lying on the bedside table. It was a note, written in a lazy scrawl. "'225 Mulberry Road.'"

"Locals already checked it out. It's a bait-and-tackle shop on the way to Douglas Lake. They're getting the security video for us, in case the Coopers made it there."

"May have nothing to do with their disappearance." Landry's tone of voice was one big shrug. She was beginning to wonder if anything interested him at all.

But not enough to ask him about it. Taciturn and antisocial was just fine with her. She wasn't exactly Susie Sunshine herself.

"We don't have a lot of time before the family shows up," Landry warned a few minutes later when they emerged from the small motel room into the late afternoon gloom. An early fall storm was rolling in from the west, advancing twilight despite the early hour. Rain would be on them soon, making the drive back to Johnson City a gloomy prospect.

"The family?" she asked.

"The Coopers. As in Cooper Security. Ever heard of it?"

"Oh. Of course." Anyone in law enforcement around these parts had heard of Cooper Security, the private agency that had brought down a major-league global conspiracy involving some of the previous administration's top people. "I thought you said this Cooper was a fisherman, though."

"He was. But Mrs. Cooper works for Cooper Security.

They'd have been informed by now, and they have access to helicopters, hell, maybe even private jets, which means they can be up in these mountains before you can say 'civilian interference in an official investigation.' No way will they stay out of this, not with both an employee and one of their own cousins gone missing."

She tried to gauge whether Landry found the thought disturbing or not. For her part, she didn't like the idea of civilians, however skilled and resourceful they might be, getting up in her business on a case. It cramped her style, if nothing else.

"Why don't we see if we can get a couple of rooms and stay here for the night?" Landry suggested, surprising her. She slanted a sharp look his way. "Territorial rights," he added with another ghost of a smile.

She smiled back. "Stake our claim?"

"Somebody's gotta do it. Might as well be us."

First sign of life she'd seen in Landry since they'd arrived. She wasn't sure if she liked it or not, but at least it suited her own intentions.

She called the resident agency and talked to Pete Chang, the Special Agent in Charge. "Do you think the case will benefit from your staying in town instead of commuting?" he asked.

"I do," she answered with more confidence than she felt.

"Approved. Just do the paperwork."

She hung up and nodded to Landry. "Go take care of getting the rooms."

His eyebrows lifted slightly. "Where are you going?"

"Just want a look around." She wandered across the parking lot, where a crowd had gathered in the deepening gloom. Onlookers were ubiquitous at any crime scene, though in a town this small, the crowd wasn't as large as it might have been in a bigger place.

She let her gaze run across the crowd, just out of habit. It had surely taken more than one person to overpower and abduct two able-bodied people, especially if one of those people was a Cooper and the other one worked for Cooper Security. Not likely they could spare someone to see what was going on at the crime scene.

But it wouldn't hurt to give the onlookers a little extra scrutiny.

Most of the people in the crowd came across as tourists rather than locals, though Ava couldn't put her finger on what, exactly, gave her that impression. She wasn't a local herself, though she was close. Her hometown was Bridal Falls, Kentucky, not far across the state line up near Jellico, Tennessee. She knew her way around the mountains.

Some of the people in this crowd weren't dressed for the mountain climate—too many clothes or not enough, depending on where they came from, she supposed. Some wore socks with sandals, which every self-respecting Southerner knew to be a big, flashing sign of an outsider. As she wandered closer to the gathered crowd, she heard a few northeastern and Midwestern accents as well, mingling with the Southern drawls.

Apparently, Landry had followed her, for his deep drawl hummed near her ear. "Is this some sort of FBI magic trick? You listening for the voice of J. Edgar or something?"

"Go get us some rooms," she repeated.

She couldn't see him, but she pictured his shrug. After his one brief moment of liveliness, he was back to the guy who didn't quite give enough of a damn about anything to put up much of an argument. He would have bugged the hell out of her last case partner, an uptight blue flamer from somewhere in the Pacific Northwest.

Didn't bother her a bit, though. A little objectiveness about a case was usually a good thing. Better than sweating every detail until you started seeing things that weren't there.

She turned away from the crowd and looked back at the motel. It was picturesque, she supposed, in the way small mountain motels were. The facade was pure sixties kitsch, complete with a space-age neon sign starting to glow bright aqua in the waning daylight. To a certain type of traveler, she supposed, the Mountain View Motor Lodge might prove too much of a temptation to resist.

Which one chose the place? she wondered. Probably the wife. This was a wife kind of place.

She noticed a truck and a high-end bass boat parked near the end of the lot. The husband was a fisherman. The boat was probably his. She pulled out her cell phone and made a note to check whether forensics had taken a look at the vehicle and the water craft.

Slipping the phone back in her pocket, she turned toward the crowd, letting her gaze slide across the faces again as she pondered the obvious question nobody had yet asked.

Why would someone kidnap a fisherman and his wife? Was it the Cooper name? Was it the wife's job at Cooper Security?

As she reached for her phone again to make a note to check into the wife's open cases, her gaze snagged on a face in the crowd.

He stood near the back, a golden-skinned face in the middle of a sea of various skin colors. Dark hair worn longer than the fashion these days lay thick and wavy around his angular features. He had a full lower lip and deep brown eyes that, back in her foolish, romantic youth, she'd thought soulful.

Someone in front of him shifted, blocking him from her view. She edged sideways, impatient, but when the space opened again, he was gone.

The electric shock coursing through her body kept zinging, however, shooting quivers along her nerve endings and sprinkling chill bumps down her arms and legs. A tidal wave of images and memories swept through her brain, washing out all good sense and replacing it with a tumble of sensations and wishes and the time-worn detritus of shattered dreams.

It's him, she thought, her heart racing like a startled deer.

Except it couldn't be him. How could it be?

Sinclair Solano was very, very dead.

UNTIL THAT BRIEF, electric clash of gazes with the woman across the motel parking lot, Sinclair Solano had almost lost touch with what it meant to be alive. He'd forgotten that something other than caution or dread could animate his pulse or spark a flood of adrenaline into his system. That his skin could tingle with pleasurable anticipation and not just the fear of discovery.

But as soon as the sensation bloomed, he crushed it with ruthless intent. He had no time for anticipation. No room for pleasure. His sister, Alicia, had disappeared from her motel room earlier that day, and while Sinclair could offer no evidence to support his theory, he knew deep in his gut—where the worst of his regrets festered—that she'd been taken because of him.

Someone in Sanselmo had discovered the truth. He hadn't died in Tesoro Harbor, as the world supposed.

And if he had not, then his former comrades would

assume only one thing: he had been their enemy, not their friend.

And enemies were not allowed to live.

The crowd shifted, and he darted back toward the woods across the sheltered road, grateful that summer's thick foliage hadn't yet surrendered to the death throes of autumn. He'd dressed today, as he had since coming to these mountains, in olive drab and camouflage, an old habit from his days with the rebels in Sanselmo. Blending into his surroundings had become second nature to him long before his "death," and nothing he'd experienced since that time had given him a reason to change.

Home these days was a lightweight weatherproof tent in the woods. He was able to pitch the tent in minutes and disassemble it as quickly as the need arose.

The only question now was: Had the need arisen again?

She'd seen him. But had she understood who she was seeing? When he'd known her, he hadn't yet crossed the line. He'd been a young man adrift, not long out of college and on a mission to find himself. Twenty-five years old, possessing a law degree but no career, a steady supply of his parents' money and a restless yearning to change the world, he'd bummed around the Caribbean for a while. Haiti for relief work. The Dominican Republic to teach English to eager young students.

The trip to Mariposa had been an oddity. A real vacation, downtime from the poverty and sadness he'd faced every day. And the pretty corn-fed college girl with her Kentucky drawl and pragmatic view of the world had seemed damned near as exotic as the Mariposan beauties.

They'd clicked, in the way opposites sometimes do, and though the smart, practical girl from Kentucky had at first been wary about being alone with a stranger on an island, they'd connected soon enough. It had been the best week of his life, a fact which had confounded him, since neither of them had done a damned thing high-minded or selfless.

Confounded him and made him feel guilty. Especially after talking to his parents one night and realizing, with dismay, that some of the things he'd found most charming about Ava had left his parents appalled and speechless.

It had been his father who'd told him about Luis Grijalva. Luis was doing amazing things in the Caribbean and South America, politically. Organizing workers, fighting for social justice, all the things that mattered to the Solano family.

The things that had mattered to Sinclair.

What was one last day with a college girl compared to meeting the great man himself and learning from his experiences?

He reached the tent, his heart still pounding, and zipped himself inside, wrapping his arms around himself to hold back the shivers. The day was mild, not cool, despite the coming storm, but he felt chilled from the inside out. He dug into the pockets of his trousers and pulled out his latest burner phone. There was a little juice left, but not much. If he didn't run in to town in the next few days, he'd be completely cut off from even the hope of communication.

He stared at the dimmed display, wondering if it was time to make contact with Quinn again. Just a call. A couple of carefully memorized code words. He hadn't tried it yet, but things had changed. Alicia was missing.

He hadn't checked in with Alexander Quinn in almost eight months. He couldn't trust that Adam Brand, the FBI agent who'd recognized him, would keep quiet. There were limits to even Quinn's influence, and enemies more powerful and ruthless than the government who'd once listed him as one of the FBI's most wanted fugitives.

But Sinclair hadn't left the mountains, either. He supposed, in a way, they were as close to a place to call home as he'd found in years of running from his past. He'd always lived in hilly places, from the rolling streets of San Francisco to the volcanic peaks of Sanselmo, the home of his heart. Even on the tiny Caribbean island of Mariposa, where he'd spent a couple of years before the call from Quinn, he'd gravitated to the mountain that filled the center of the island.

The Smoky Mountains were an alpine rainforest rather than a tropical one. But they'd felt like a place of refuge ever since he'd arrived.

Until now.

THOUGH SHE'D GROWN UP in the mountains, it had been a while since Ava had spent much time in the middle of unfettered nature. She'd been living in cities for several years now, where hiking meant leaving the Ford Focus at home instead of driving it downhill to the grocery store when she had a few things to pick up.

But she'd stayed fit, thanks to the demands of her job, and she found some of her old childhood skills coming back to her as she picked her way through the thickening forest.

The land sloped gently upward, making her calves burn as she hiked, but she shrugged the twinges away, concentrating instead on trying to follow the trail through the gloom. Rain had started to fall by the time she reached a fork in the forest trail, turning her hair to damp, frizzled curls beneath the hood of her jacket.

She should have been shocked that Landry hadn't asked more questions about why she was heading into the woods, but based on her hours in his unadulterated presence, she wasn't surprised at all. He was phoning it in these days, for whatever reason. She doubted he'd last at the agency much longer with that attitude. But she didn't have the time or the inclination to dig deeper into what drove him to such epic levels of ennui.

She had an abduction to solve, and based on what she'd learned from her supervisory agent just a few minutes earlier, chasing a ghost into the woods just might be the best use of her time.

"Don't know if it means anything," SAC Chang had told her when he'd called, "but her name pinged in our records because of her familial connection to a terrorist."

At that point, she'd known who the terrorist would be. Hadn't she?

She certainly hadn't been surprised to hear him add, "Her maiden name is Solano."

Sinclair Solano's sister had gone missing the same day Ava had looked up into the crowd at the crime scene and seen the ghost of her brother. And since she didn't believe in ghosts, there was only one explanation.

Sinclair Solano was alive after all.

"Come on, Sin," she muttered, blinking away a film of rain blurring her vision even as it darkened the day. "Where the hell did you go?"

The man she'd met years earlier, before his descent into murder and mayhem, had been a real charmer. Handsome, beautifully tanned, in love with beauty and music and passionate about the world of people around him, he'd been as exotic to her as a Mariposan native, even though he was an American, born and raised in San Francisco. His parents were college professors, he'd told her. His sister was a brainiac who'd skipped grades and was already on the verge of graduating from college at the age of twenty.

He'd liked her accent, argued passionately with some of her politics without making her feel evil or stupid and when he'd kissed her, she would have sworn she heard music.

How he'd gone from that man to the scourge of Sanselmo was a mystery that had nagged her for a long time, until word of his death had reached the news shortly after the terrorist bomb blast he'd set, one intended to take out the new president and his family, went terribly wrong for him and some of his comrades instead.

She was glad, she'd told herself. Poetic justice and all that.

But there was a part of her that had always felt cheated. That curious part of her, the one that had driven her into her current job, that wanted to know why.

Why had he blown her off that last day in Mariposa, knowing her flight would leave the next morning? Why had he grown so cold and distant after talking to his father on the phone?

Why had he left Mariposa for Sanselmo, armed himself on the side of brutal, ruthless rebels and channeled his passion for justice into a murderous assault on a nascent democratic republic?

After word of his death, she'd resigned herself to never knowing the answers to those nagging questions.

Now maybe she'd get a chance to ask them after all.

The rain fell harder around her, seeping under the collar of her jacket. Her trousers were soaked through and beginning to chafe. Worst of all, she had no damned idea where she was anymore. And if the ghost she was chasing had left any sort of trail from here forward, she saw no sign of it.

Trudging to a stop, she just stood still a moment, listening to the woods, taking in the ambient sounds—the susurration of rainfall, the distant hum of engines from the highway north of her position, the slightly ragged whoosh of her own breathing.

Another sound seeped into her consciousness. Footsteps. Careful. Furtive.

Turning a slow circle, she let her gaze go unfocused. Let the wall of green become a blur against which movement might become more evident. She slowed her breathing deliberately, remembering lessons from the shooting classes she'd taken in pursuit of her career, determined to be the best at any task she took on. Her own weapon, a Glock G30S, sat heavily in the small of her back. She reached behind her slowly and eased it from the holster.

She wasn't dressed for stealth on purpose, but her brown jacket, olive-green blouse and dark trousers didn't make her an easy target. She had ordinary brown hair, not a bright shock of red curls that might draw attention her way. Plain olive-toned skin, unlikely to stand out in the gloom. She was in many ways a nondescript woman, which had served her well on the job.

But right now, she felt utterly exposed as the crackle of underbrush filtered through the patter of rainfall.

Someone was watching her. She felt it.

Edging back in the direction she came, she tried not to panic. Coming out here alone had been reckless, especially when she probably could have convinced Landry to come along with her if she'd made the effort.

She hadn't wanted to tell him what she'd seen. That was the truth of the matter. She hadn't wanted to see his skepticism or, worse, his ridicule. Didn't want to hear that she was imagining things.

She knew what she'd seen. She'd looked at Sinclair's photograph for years, even after his death, wondering how the sweet-natured, passionate man she'd met in the Caribbean could have become a terrorist.

The wind picked up, swirling leaves from the trees to slap her rain-stung cheeks. Blinking away a film of moisture, she quickened her steps.

A dark mass rose out of the gloom to her right, slamming into her with a jarring blow before she could react. She staggered against the impact, trying to keep her feet, but shoes slipped on the rain-slick leaves carpeting the forest floor and she hit the ground. Her pistol went flying in the underbrush, out of reach. Breath whooshed from her lungs, and her vision darkened to a narrow tunnel of blurry light.

Rough hands grabbed at her as she gasped for air. Twisting, she tried to see her captor, certain she would see Sinclair Solano's face staring back at her. But the dark-eyed man who held her in his painful grasp was someone she'd never seen before.

He shoved his pistol into the soft flesh beneath her chin, the front sight digging painfully into her skin. "*¡Silencio!*"

Her pulse rattling in her throat, she had no choice but to comply.

Chapter Two

It had happened in the span of a couple of seconds. One second, Ava Trent been turning back toward the path that had brought her within sight. The next, a man in the familiar jungle camouflage pattern of an *El Cambio* rebel had risen from behind a thick mountain laurel bush and slammed into her like a linebacker. They'd both gone down, but Ava had taken the brunt of the impact, struggling to breathe as the man grabbed her up and jammed a pistol under her chin.

Sin's heart hammered in terror as he scanned the area for an accomplice. There. Emerging from the trees, a second man glided into view, grabbing Ava by the arm.

Two against one, with Ava as the wild card. She'd been carrying a weapon, and back at the crime scene she'd been moving about like a woman with a purpose. Law enforcement, maybe? She'd been circumspect about what she'd be doing when she returned home from vacation, but some things she'd said had hinted at a police job.

Had she recognized him across the parking lot and come out here to find him?

He was armed because Quinn had told him he'd be stupid to walk around unprotected. But despite his reputation, he wasn't a man comfortable with violence. He never had been.

But he could be, under the right circumstances. He'd learned that much about himself in Sanselmo.

Pulling the pistol from the hidden holster inside his jacket, he wished he had a rifle instead. Better accuracy from a distance. But the Taurus 1911 would do.

Across the woods, the man holding the pistol to Ava's chin drew his hand back, bringing the pistol muzzle away from her face. But as he did so, the second man grabbed her from behind in a bear hug, eliciting a grunt of surprise from her as she started to struggle against his hold.

The man with the gun pressed it to her forehead, and Sin aimed the Taurus in his direction, his finger sliding onto the trigger.

Ava slumped suddenly, her arms sliding up and her body dropping, catching the man holding her by surprise. She slipped from his grasp, down to the forest floor.

Sinclair would never get a better chance.

Aiming down the barrel of the Taurus, he fired. Simultaneously, another shot rang out, the crack echoing in the trees, almost drowning out the report of his own weapon. The man reaching for Ava fell backward into the underbrush. The man in front of her pitched forward, firing off a shot of his own as he fell.

Ava's body jerked, even as she rolled away from the falling man, scrambled to her feet and started running. She made it about ten yards before she started to stagger, her legs wobbling beneath her as if they'd gone boneless. She fell forward into the thickening underbrush, disappearing from his view.

Keeping an eye on the two fallen men, Sinclair dashed after her, his heart racing faster than his churning legs. She lay crumpled, facedown, but he could see by the rise and fall of her body that she was still breathing. He stopped next to the two fallen men. The one who'd grabbed Ava first lay facedown, unmoving. The back of his camouflage jacket had a bloody hole in it, somewhere in the vicinity of his left shoulder blade. He didn't appear to be breathing. Nudging with his foot, Sin rolled the man over and took a long look at his face.

Emilio Fuentes, he thought, staring into the glassy brown eyes of a man he'd once called friend. His heart contracted.

He picked up the pistol Fuentes had dropped and shoved it into his pocket. He checked the second man, the one at whom he'd aimed his own pistol. Carlito Escalante. A bloody hole in the side of the man's neck was the only obvious injury. Sin checked for a pulse and found none.

A queasy sensation filled his gut, and he swallowed the urge to be sick.

He searched Carlito's body, found a hunting knife besides the pistol the man had dropped, and added both to his pocket, trying not to let his rapid respirations escalate to hyperventilation. He needed his wits about him. His life had just gotten a thousand times more dangerous.

By the time he found the pistol Ava had dropped when she was attacked and turned back to her, she was on her hands and knees, trying to crawl away. He hurried to her side, crouching beside her.

She whirled at his touch, swinging her arm up in a shaky arc before he could react. Suddenly, he was staring down the muzzle of a Glock aimed right between his eyes. Now he knew where the second shot had come from.

She'd had another weapon.

"Ava," he said.

"You're supposed to be dead." Her voice had a raw, uneven tone, the shaking in her hand growing to an alarming wobble.

He reached out and moved her hand away from his

face. She struggled but didn't pull the trigger before he took the gun away and wrapped his arm around her as she started to fall backward. "Whoa, there." Dropping the Glock to one side, he gave her a quick appraisal, looking for her injury.

There. Under the hem of her jacket. Blood spread across the right side of her charcoal trousers and seeped upward onto her olive-green blouse. As she tried to slap his hands away, he tugged the blouse up and away, revealing a ripped furrow in the waistband of her pants. Beneath it, the bullet's path had carved a bloody gouge in the soft flesh just above her hip bone.

"Ow," she groaned as he plucked a piece of scorched fabric from the wound.

He needed to get her back to the motel. And he needed not to get caught. Irreconcilable goals.

"You didn't blow yourself up," she muttered. He looked up from the bullet wound to find her hazel eyes focused on his face.

"Says who?" he asked, reaching in his back pocket for his multibladed knife. There was a set of tweezers tucked into the handle, if he wasn't mistaken. Given the messy condition of her wound, he was probably going to need them.

"You're wanted by the FBI."

"I'm not on the list anymore," he disagreed, sliding the tweezers out. "Dead, you see."

Her mouth twisted with frustration. "You're not dead. And you're under arrest."

He couldn't hold back a grin at her serious expression. "Can I finish cleaning this wound before you take me in?"

"This isn't funny." Moving more quickly than he thought she could, she grabbed the Glock he'd taken from her and swung it back in front of her. This time, her hands didn't shake nearly as hard.

Fear battled with grudging admiration. She was tougher than she looked. "What are you going to do, shoot me?"

"If I have to."

"Getting back to the motel on your own isn't going to be pleasant," he warned, sitting back on his heels.

"I'll deal." Keeping her pistol aimed at his chest, she pushed to her feet, struggling not to sway. "Sinclair Solano, you're under arrest for the murder of three American oil company employees. For starters."

"I didn't kill those men."

"We'll let the courts sort that out." She twitched the Glock's muzzle at him. "Move."

He wasn't going to let her take him in. He'd had his chance to face justice years ago and had traded it for a chance to make things right. But Alexander Quinn had warned him there were no easy outs. Once he went back to *El Cambio* and pretended nothing had changed, he might never be able to clear his name.

He'd taken the chance. Now, it seemed he might have to pay.

"Do you know who those men were?" He nodded toward the two bodies lying several yards away.

Her gaze slanted toward them briefly before locking with Sin's again. "No. Do you?"

"The one who grabbed you was Emilio Fuentes. Major player in *El Cambio*'s military wing. He was Alberto Cabrera's top commander." He watched her expression for any signs of recognition. Her eyes narrowed; she knew something about *El Cambio,* he thought. "The other was Carlito Escalante."

"The Spider," she murmured, recognition dawning.

She wasn't just playing at whatever job she was working, clearly, if she knew Escalante's nom de guerre. He tried not to stare into the muzzle of her Glock. "Why do you suppose two of *El Cambio*'s top enforcers were wandering around the Smoky Mountains?"

"They're looking for you."

He gave a brief nod. "They're looking for me."

"Why?"

"Because I'm not one of them. Because I betrayed them a long time ago, and somehow, they figured out I'm not dead."

Her eyes narrowed in her pain-creased face. "Betrayed them how?"

"Long story, *carida.* Remind me to tell you about it sometime."

"Are there others out here?"

He suspected there were. If Cabrera had sent two enforcers, he'd probably sent a dozen. The arrogant son of a bitch had never economized on anything. "The motel is about a mile in that direction," he said, nodding toward the northwest. "But I can't promise you won't run into more like those two."

Her nostrils flared, the only sign of reaction to his words. "Or maybe you're just telling me that so I'll let you go."

He shrugged. "Your call."

She pushed painfully to her feet, keeping the pistol barrel pointed at his chest. "Walk."

"I'm not going back to the motel with you, so you might as well shoot me now."

A muscle in her jaw twitched dangerously. "Why did you even come back here? You had to know you'd be arrested if anyone ever found you."

"There's a man named Alexander Quinn." Her forehead creased slightly with recognition, so he proceeded without further explanation. "He recruited me years ago. Not long after I joined up with *El Cambio.*"

"Recruited you for what?"

A flash in the gloom behind her distracted him. It was quick, but his instincts were honed for action after all these years living on the edge of the razor. He threw himself at her, praying she wouldn't shoot before he knocked her to the ground.

A sharp report shattered the air around them. It took a moment for him to realize it had come from the woods, not from her pistol.

He held her down, lifting his head just enough to peer through the underbrush for more signs of movement. Beneath his body, she wriggled, her breath coming in short, pained gasps.

"Shh," he whispered, dropping his head back below the underbrush.

"Was that—?" Her words came out in a raspy wheeze.

"Someone shooting at us?" he whispered, shifting to give her room to breathe. "Yes. Yes, it was."

RAIN NEEDLED HER FACE, soft prickles she could barely feel. All of her senses seemed gathered on the burning ache of her torn flesh and the dizzying sensation of Sinclair Solano's very warm, very alive body covering hers. She expected more gunfire, but it didn't come.

"They didn't just leave," she whispered, hating that she was on her back, blind to the angle of attack. But moving more than an inch or two might make them easier targets. Sometimes, waiting for a more advantageous situation was the only reasonable option.

Not that she had to like it.

"I know." Sin edged slowly to one side. As the weight of his body eased from hers, she sucked in a deeper breath.

Almost immediately, she wished she hadn't, as the rise and fall of her diaphragm tugged the skin around her wound.

Biting her lip, she carefully rolled to her side. The movement brought her close to Sin again, but she had a better view of the woods in front of them. "There could be people coming from all directions."

"I know."

She had held on to the spare Glock, she realized with a twinge of surprise. For a few moments there, when he'd slammed her to the ground, all she'd been aware of was gutting pain. She eased the pistol forward, trying not to rustle the tangle of undergrowth that hid their position.

"If we can get back to the motel, we'll have backup," she added, slanting a look at him. "Want to rethink the whole resisting arrest thing?"

"I'm not guilty of murder."

She couldn't tell if he was lying or not. It sounded like the truth, but his gaze slanted away from hers as he said it.

"And you're willing to die to avoid defending yourself?"

"Where's your cell phone?" he asked.

She almost banged her head on the ground in frustration. What the hell? Why hadn't she already pulled out her phone and called in the cavalry?

As she dropped her hand to her right pocket, her palm grazed the wound over her hip, and she sucked in a hiss of breath. Biting her lip, she reached into her pocket and pulled out the phone.

It was in pieces. The bullet had apparently hit the metal phone case and deflected into her hip. But not before it smashed into the phone itself, cracking it in two.

She looked at Sin. "Don't suppose you'd lend me yours?"

He shook his head. "I'm not letting you take me in."

"Then I guess we both die out here." Grinding her teeth in anger, she lifted her head briefly, long enough to see above the underbrush. Movement to the south caught her attention, and she ducked again. "They're circling around to the south."

"Maybe checking on Fuentes and Escalante."

She turned her head toward him, her heart freezing for a long, dizzying moment as she realized he gripped a large Taurus 1911, a shiny silver monster of a pistol with a walnut grip.

His gaze met hers. "I'm not going to shoot you." He nodded toward the south. "Might shoot him, though."

She followed his gaze and saw a man dressed in dark green camouflage moving quietly through the underbrush. The same man who'd already shot at them? Or someone new? She wasn't sure.

"How do we get out of here?" she whispered, trying to ignore the burning pain in her hip. If she crouched here much longer in one position, she wasn't sure she'd be able to move when the time came.

"We need a distraction," he murmured.

"Got any ideas?"

"Yeah, one, but I should have pulled the trigger on that option about thirty minutes ago," he answered, his gaze still on the man creeping through the gloom in front of them. "Too late now."

A streak of lightning lit the sky overhead, and the man in camouflage jerked in reaction, especially when a booming crash of thunder followed only a second later.

"Just great," Ava muttered. As if the rain wasn't enough.

"Just might be," Sin said quietly.

She glanced at him. He was still watching the other man, his eyes narrowed in thought.

"What are you thinking?" she asked, uneasy at how

quickly they'd gone from opponents to allies with the addition of the new intruder. She'd do well to remember that, no matter what help Sinclair Solano might be offering at the moment, he was still a wanted man. He was suspected in over a dozen terrorist bombings in Sanselmo, many of which had killed innocent civilians—men, women and even children.

But Sin wasn't the one hunting her now, so she had to be pragmatic about the situation. He seemed to know where he was and what he was doing. And she was bleeding and growing stiffer by the minute.

Another flash of lightning cracked open the sky. This time, the thunder sounded right on its heels, stopping the man hunting them in his tracks. Ava took the opportunity for a quick look around for more men in camouflage. She didn't see anyone else out there, but Sin was probably right. If Cabrera had bothered to send two of his top lieutenants to look for Sin, he'd have sent more than just three people. There might be a whole squad of killers roaming these woods.

Getting out of here wasn't going to be easy.

"Next flash of lightning, I want you to run east, as fast as you can. Due east. About two hundred yards in that direction, you'll find a tent covered with a Ghillie net. Get inside and be ready to shoot anyone who sticks his head inside."

She shot him a look. "Even you?"

"I'll say, 'Alicia is missing,' and you'll know it's me."

"Alicia is missing?" she repeated, not sure if it was smart to admit she knew the connection between her kidnapping victim and the man beside her.

"She is, isn't she?" His throat bobbed as he turned his gaze toward the man still creeping through the trees.

"Cabrera's people almost certainly have her. They took her as a way to put pressure on me."

"Why would they think it would?" she asked, wondering if he'd tell her the truth.

"Because Alicia Cooper's maiden name is Solano."

"Your sister?"

He looked at her oddly. "You already knew that."

She didn't deny it.

He sighed. "I have to find her before they do something that can't be reversed."

"She's with her husband. He'll help protect her."

Sinclair nodded. "If they don't kill him first."

Lightning streaked across the sky, one jagged crack after another. Thunder rolled in a continuous roar, and Sin gave her a nudge. "Now!"

She reversed position, clamping her teeth together as pain raced through her side to settle in a raw burn at the point of her hip. Staying low, she raced east. Or, at least, what she hoped was east. She heard a commotion behind her, gunshots stuttering through the drumbeat of rain.

Head down, she ran faster, deeper into the woods. Pain squeezed tears from her eyes, but she couldn't slow down. Footsteps crashed through the underbrush behind her, but she didn't look back.

The Ghillie shelter rose up in the gloom so quickly, she almost ran headfirst into the tent. Spotting the opening, she wriggled into the small tent and turned until she sat facing front, her knees pulled up to her chest despite the howl of pain from her torn hip. She held her Glock steady by using her knees as a shooting rest, willing her heartbeat to slow and her ragged respiration to even out.

Alicia is missing, she thought, trying to piece together the disparate shards of information she'd gleaned over the past half hour. Alicia Cooper was originally Alicia Solano.

Sinclair's sister. Chang had told her that much. But did Alicia know her brother was alive? Did she know why Cabrera's men had taken her and her husband?

Was Gabe Cooper even alive?

"Alicia is missing." Even without the code words, she recognized Sinclair Solano's voice. "I'm coming in."

The flap of the tent opened. She tightened her grip on the Glock, her trigger finger sliding down from where she'd held it flattened against the side of the pistol. She tried not to hold her breath, but air wouldn't seem to move in or out of her lungs while she waited for him to appear.

Then, in the space of a blink, he was there, crawling inside the tent, little more than a dark shadow within the darker confines of the shelter.

"Are you okay?" he asked, his voice barely a whisper.

"I think so."

"I shot a third man when he shot at me. He's dead. But there are others out there. I heard them calling to one another."

She pressed one hand to her mouth, feeling sick. "And we're sitting ducks in this tent."

"We're under shelter. There are alarms outside to let us know if intruders are getting close." He reached for a blanket that lay beside her on the tent floor. She hadn't even noticed it, hadn't realized how hard she was shivering until he draped it over her shoulders. Warmth rolled over her like a wave, driving out some of the chills.

"Better?" he asked.

She nodded. "I didn't notice any alarms outside."

"You wouldn't have," he said with a quirk of a smile. He hunkered down next to her, sticking close enough that the searing heat of his body was as good as a blazing fire. The only thing missing was the comfort of light. The tent remained dark and would only get darker as night continued to fall.

"So what now?" she whispered.

He blew out a long, slow breath. "We wait out the storm and hope those fellows don't find us."

Chapter Three

As plans went, waiting and hoping weren't high on Sinclair's list of great ones. But his burner phone had no juice left. He'd have to get to civilization to charge the phone, and even then, he wasn't sure what, if anything, Alexander Quinn could do to help him find Alicia and her husband.

"I need to go back to the motel," Ava said after a few moments of tense silence. "I have work to do."

"You're a cop?"

She gave him a strange look, then released a soft huff of breath that was almost a laugh. "Oh, right. I left the other jacket in the car."

"What other jacket?"

He could barely make out the curve of her pained smile. "The blue jacket with the big yellow *FBI* on the back."

"FBI." Great. Of all the old acquaintances he could have run into in the middle of the woods, he had to run into the one who worked for the federal agency that had once had his face tacked prominently to every wall of every field office and resident agency in the country.

"We think you're dead, you know. Well, everyone *else* does."

"I'd love for it to stay that way."

"Too bad. I'm not your friend, Solano. I can't look the other way. So if you're going to kill me to stop me from ratting on you, go for it now so one or the other of us can get on with trying to stay alive."

"I'm not what you think I am." He sighed as she gave him a look so skeptical he couldn't miss it even in the near darkness. "I know you've probably heard that before."

"You reckon?"

"There's a lot you don't know."

"Let me guess. You were really a double agent working for the CIA to bring down *El Cambio* from the inside." Her sarcasm had a sharp bite.

Well, he thought. *There goes the truth as a viable explanation.*

Awkward silence descended between them again. Strange, Sin thought, how hard it was to talk to her now, when back in Mariposa, all those years ago, talking to Ava Trent had seemed as easy as breathing.

She'd been nothing like any girl he'd ever known, growing up in San Francisco, and he supposed maybe the sheer novelty of her had been the initial attraction. That and her curvy little figure, displayed not in a skin-baring bikini, but a trim racer-back one-piece, standing out on the Mariposan beach amid all those skimpy thongs and barely-there tops. She'd swum the ocean as if it were a sport, tackling waves with ferocity of purpose, all flexing muscles and determination.

Somehow, her lack of self-consciousness about her appearance had only made her more attractive in Sinclair's eyes. And when she'd opened her mouth and that Kentucky drawl had meandered out, he'd been leveled completely. There had been no other word for the way she'd made him feel, as if the earth beneath his feet had liquefied and he couldn't hold a solid thought in his head.

She'd declared he'd like Kentucky, if he was looking

for somewhere new to visit. And he'd almost talked himself into going back there with her.

"How sure are you that it's Cabrera who has your sister?" Ava's whisper broke the tense silence filling the tent.

"Pretty sure," he answered. "Do you have evidence to the contrary?"

She was silent for a moment. "I just got here this afternoon. I didn't have a lot of time to investigate before I went on a ghost hunt."

Feeling her gaze on him in the gloom, he turned his head to find her watching him, eyes glittering. "I didn't think anyone would see me."

"How'd you find out about the kidnapping?"

"I heard the sirens." Reliving that heart-sinking moment when he'd realized all those lights and sirens had been headed for the motel where his sister was staying, he struggled to breathe. "I'd seen a write-up in the local paper about a visit from a previous bass tournament champion. Her husband, Gabe. There was a picture of the two of them, right on the front page of the sports section."

Alicia had looked so beautiful in that photo, he thought. So happy. The guy she'd married seemed solid, too. Quinn had told him a few things about the Coopers, whom Quinn knew through prior dealings with the family. Gabe Cooper had been among the family members who'd done battle with a South American drug lord seeking vengeance against one of the Coopers. Sinclair prayed he'd be just as strong in protecting Alicia.

Of course, Cabrera's men might have executed him the first chance they got. They were nothing if not ruthless.

"They're keeping her alive," Ava murmured. "There's no point in killing her if they want to use her to smoke you out."

"I may have done the job for them."

"Three dead and we're still at large. That's not nothing." Her voice had grown progressively more strained. That wound she'd suffered was probably hurting like hell by now.

"I need to take a look at your wound."

"It's okay."

"It needs to be cleaned out and disinfected. The longer we wait to do that, the more likely infection will set in." It might not be possible to avoid infection even now, but it wouldn't hurt to clean her up. "I have first aid supplies."

"We can't risk a light."

"The Ghillie cover will block most of it, and the woods should take care of the rest, unless they stumble right on us. And if that happens, the light will be the least of our worries."

She released a gusty sigh. "Okay. But be quick."

He grabbed his bag from the back of the tent and pulled out the compact first-aid kit. Fortunately, he'd stocked up a few days ago when he'd made a run to Bentwood to charge his burner phone. Using a penlight to see what he was doing, he pulled out disinfectant, gauze, tape and a couple of ibuprofen tablets to help her with the pain. The kit also offered a bigger pair of tweezers. One look at the messy furrow ripped into the fleshy part of her hip suggested he was going to have to do some careful work to get all the singed fabric out of the wound.

"I'd offer you a bullet to bite," he said, keeping his voice light, "but we may need to conserve them."

"Just get it done." She pushed down her trousers, wincing as the fabric stuck to the drying blood at the edges of her wound.

He handed her the penlight. "Can you hold this for me?"

She positioned the light over her hip, turning her head away and burying it in the elbow crook of her other arm.

He worked quickly, wincing at her soft grunts of pain. The wound was about five inches long and at least a half-inch deep, grooving a path right through the flesh of her hip. It had missed the bone, fortunately, and she had enough curves for the bullet to have also missed most of the muscle. "Looks like it mostly injured fatty tissue," he commented as he dabbed antiseptic along the margins of the wound.

"I'm suddenly feeling less guilty about that chocolate-covered doughnut I had for breakfast," she mumbled.

"We need to get you somewhere cleaner than these woods," he said as he bandaged up the wound.

"I'm counting on that," she answered. "You'll be coming, too."

"I can't do that."

"You don't get a vote."

He looked down at her bared hip, the utter vulnerability of her current pose. "You're in no position to make demands at the moment."

She moved as quickly as a cat, the grimace on her face as she whipped up to face him betraying the pain the move caused her. Still, she had her Glock in his face before he could put down the first aid kit. "Want to bet?"

He couldn't stop a smile, even though he knew it would only make her angry. "You'll have to shoot me, then."

Her lips pressed to a thin line. "Why aren't you dead, Solano?"

"Because I never walked into that warehouse in Tesoro with the rest of the crew." He tamped down the memories—the thunderous bomb blast, the sickening knowledge that people he knew, people he'd lived with and sometimes even liked, were gone, martyrs to a cause he'd once embraced and now despised.

"The authorities in Sanselmo accounted for your body."

"There were ten bodies. Mine just wasn't one of them."

"You killed someone to fake your own death?"

"He was already dead. John Doe from the local morgue."

"You knew those men would die when they went in there. Why would you betray your own comrades that way? I never thought you were amoral. Wrong? Absolutely. Following a fool's path? Certainly. But to kill nine men to fake your own death?"

"It wasn't my doing," he said, not sure how much he should reveal to her about what he'd done all those years ago. Some of it was probably still classified. He and Quinn had never discussed what he would have to tell the world if he were ever caught.

"Don't get caught" had been Quinn's oh-so-helpful advice.

Besides, she had already dismissed the truth as a possible explanation. What good would it do to tell her at this point?

"If it wasn't your doing, whose was it?"

He took a deep breath. "I can't say. There are other people involved. Some of them might still be in dangerous situations."

Her eyes narrowed. "So you're going with the 'secret CIA double agent' story after all? Really?"

He looked away from those sharp eyes, his gaze falling to her midsection, where her unbuttoned trousers were riding down perilously, revealing black panties, the luscious curve of her hips and the sleek plane of her flat belly. His body responded fiercely, a white-hot ache settling low in his groin. It had been a damned long time since he'd been this close to a woman. And this woman, in particular, had gotten under his skin in record time once before.

Clearly, in the eight years since, he hadn't developed an immunity.

He cleared his throat and waved his hand toward her open fly. "You're about to lose your britches."

As she glanced down, he grabbed her wrist, moving the muzzle of her Glock away from his face. Her gaze flew up to meet his, her expression shifting between mortification and anger. But not fear, he noticed. For whatever reason, she didn't seem to fear him.

Lust flared like fire in his belly.

He let go of her wrist. "I told you, I'm not going to hurt you. But I don't like having a gun in my face."

She jerked back from him, but she didn't aim her gun his way again, he noticed with relief. When she spoke, her voice was soft and raspy. "How did you get out of Sanselmo without being caught? How did you make it back here to the States, for that matter?"

"Same answer to both questions. I had help."

"From whom?"

"The good guys."

"Good guys in whose eyes?" Her tone was acerbic.

"Interesting question, that."

"CIA, I suppose?" She looked disappointed that he wasn't coming up with a different story.

Too bad, he thought. *You may not like it. Hell, I didn't like it much myself. But the truth is what it is.*

"I'm going to take a look outside. I think it's dark enough to risk it." He turned in the narrow confines of the tent and started crawling toward the exit. As he neared the flap, he felt the heat of her body scrambling up behind him. She nudged her way to his side, her body soft and sizzling hot against his. Another flare of desire bolted through him, making his arms and legs tremble.

He turned to look at her. Her small, heart-shaped face

turned toward his, her eyes large and dark in the faint ambient light coming from outside. “This doesn’t require us both,” he murmured.

“I’m not letting you out of my sight.”

She was going to make his quest to find his sister a little more difficult, he realized. Because if there was one thing he’d learned about Ava Trent during that week they’d spent together in Mariposa, it was the depth of her sheer, dogged determination. She attacked every task she took on with the same pedal-to-the-floorboard pluck.

She wouldn’t be easy to shake. And he wasn’t going to hurt her.

So how did he plan to proceed?

The easy answer would be to somehow make her an ally rather than an enemy. But short of spilling a boatload of long-held state secrets, how was he supposed to do that? And would she believe him even if he told her every little piece of the truth?

He needed to talk to Quinn, which meant heading for the closest town to charge his burner phone. And the closest town was Poe Creek, about a mile through the *El Cambio*–infested woods. Poe Creek, where cops still swarmed about the motel crime scene. Where Ava probably had fellow agents beginning to wonder where the hell she’d disappeared to and whether it was time to call for reinforcements to go looking for her.

“How many people are with you?” he asked.

She frowned. “I’m not going to tell you that.”

“They’ll be looking for you. Don’t want to shoot the wrong people.”

“You won’t be shooting anyone,” she said firmly.

“We’ve already shot three people trying to kill us. I’m not going to stop trying to defend myself—or you—just because you've decided to make your name as an FBI agent on my bounty."

She made a low, growling sound thick with frustration. "I don't want to shoot you."

"Good to know."

"But you're a fugitive from justice, and bringing you in is my job."

"Why don't we concentrate on getting out of these woods alive first?" he suggested, trying to sound reasonable. The grumble that escaped her throat at his words suggested he hadn't entirely succeeded.

But she gave a short nod toward the tent flap in response. "Think they're still out there, then?"

"Somewhere," he affirmed. "But now that we know they're looking for me, we can be more careful moving through the woods. I think we can stay a step ahead of them until we get back to civilization."

At least, he hoped they could. Because one way or another, he needed to get word to Alexander Quinn. The spymaster had warned him something like this might happen.

Every man's sin sooner or later came back to haunt him.

HER HIP WAS burning like fire, the pain as effective as a cup of strong coffee to keep her heart pounding and her adrenaline pumping. Without the pain, she might have been tempted to hunker down and wait for daylight, because sneaking through the woods at night was harder than she remembered.

She had grown up in a rural area, traipsed through her share of woods and mountains, but rarely at night, and never with five inches of bullet-grazed flesh playing a symphony of agony with each careful step. But, as she reminded herself in a silent litany as she followed Sinclair Solano through a tangle of underbrush, each step took them closer to civilization. Closer to a clean bandage, prescription antibiotics and painkillers.

Closer to the safety of numbers.

She had come to the conclusion that Sin was being honest about one thing—he didn't intend to kill her, even if she tried to take him into actual custody instead of this parody of custody they were playing out at the moment. But that didn't mean he wouldn't try to stop her.

He'd been at this fugitive thing a long time. Clearly, he was good at it.

So the ball was in her court, she supposed. He might not be willing to kill her to maintain his freedom, but was she willing to kill him if he resisted her attempt to keep him in her custody? Was she willing to let Cade Landry shoot him? Or one of the local cops?

This shouldn't even be a question, Trent. You're an FBI agent. Taking criminals into custody is part of what you do.

But Sinclair Solano had saved her life. Put his own life at risk to do it. And when he swore he wasn't the man she thought he was, he seemed to believe what he was saying.

Her boot tangled with a thick root somewhere beneath the mass of vines, scrub and decaying leaves underfoot, tipping her off balance. She stumbled forward, grabbing for something, anything to break her fall.

She slammed into the hard, solid heat of Sin's chest as he moved quickly to catch her. His arms roped around her body, holding her close, lifting her back to her feet.

He didn't let go immediately, his breath hot against her cheek. Despite the pain in her side, despite the adrenaline still flooding her body, she felt an answering rush of heat racing through her veins to settle, heavy and liquid, in the juncture of her thighs.

She wasn't twenty and carefree, enjoying her last taste

of freedom before law school and the FBI career she'd chosen for herself. These woods weren't the cool, lush rainforest surrounding the soaring peak of Mt. Stanley.

And Sinclair Solano had long since ceased to be just some sexy, brooding fellow tourist who'd made her pulse race and her toes tingle with a few hot kisses under the Mariposa moon.

He let her go slowly, his hands sliding down her arms, his fingers brushing hers lightly as he released her. "You okay?" he whispered.

Her voice felt trapped in her throat. She nodded without attempting to free it.

For a long, electric moment, he continued gazing at her. Apparently, Poe Creek had not yet folded up its streets for the night, for faint light glowed in the west, edging his features with a hint of gold. He had tawny skin and dark, dark eyes, and eight years past their brief entanglement, his compelling magnetism still tugged at her unwilling heart.

"What am I going to do with you?" he asked, and she realized with a shiver those exact words were echoing in her own troubled mind.

"Tell me the truth." She couldn't stop herself from taking a step closer, as if he'd tugged an invisible cord between them. "If you tell the truth, I'll know it. And I'll know what to do. Why did you join *El Cambio?* And why did you leave?"

For a tense moment, he stared at her, his expression unreadable. Then, as he opened his mouth to answer, a loud crack sounded from close by.

She dropped, grabbing his arm and dragging him down with her. Adrenaline spiked, sending her heart into a wild gallop as she tried to find cover in the underbrush, her gaze darting around the darkened woods in search of the intruder.

"That wasn't a gunshot," Sin whispered, his face close enough that his breath tickled the tendrils of hair curling on her forehead.

"What was it?"

Before he could answer, a flurry of sound and movement broke the tense quiet of the woods. Thirty yards to the north, two men burst into view out of the underbrush, scrambling and stumbling as they went, throwing fearful looks behind them.

A few yards behind them, a large black bear loped after them, moving with surprising speed.

"I thought black bears didn't attack unprovoked," she whispered, watching the animal crash through the forest after the two fleeing men.

"She may have a cub around here somewhere."

One of the men seemed to finally remember he was armed. He swung his gun hand toward the bear and fired a shot. It missed the bear, the bullet whipping through a thicket only ten yards away from where Ava and Sin crouched.

Sin grabbed her around the waist and hauled her with him behind a nearby tree trunk. The sudden movement pulled at her injury, and she hissed with pain.

"Sorry!" he whispered in her ear, sliding his hand up to her rib cage.

But he didn't let her go.

Another gunshot rang in the woods. Another bullet missed the bear and whizzed harmlessly past their hiding place by a dozen yards. The next time Ava peeked around the tree trunk, the bear was circling back around, heading away from where they crouched. The men were two diminishing shadows in the woods, still on the run.

Ava released a long breath. "That was close. Let's get out of here."

"Wait," Sin murmured, catching her arm as she started to move.

She looked up at him, jerking her arm free of his grip. "What?"

He met her gaze, his eyes burning with fierce intent. "We have to follow those men."

Chapter Four

Clearly, she thought he was crazy. Hell, maybe he was—those men were probably better armed and equipped than either of them, and he had no idea how many of them might be roaming the woods at the moment.

"We need to go back to the motel and report those guys," she said firmly, starting westward.

He caught up with her, taking care not to touch her this time. "The bear scared the hell out of those guys. I'd bet they're heading back to wherever Cabrera has set up camp in these hills. This could be our best chance to find out where that is." His voice went raspy as emotion tightened his throat. "They might lead us to my sister."

Her gaze softened. "They're already out of sight."

"I can track them. I've had a lot of experience in the past few years."

Pinching her lower lip between her teeth, she gazed toward the darkness where the two men had disappeared. She released a huff of breath. "Okay, you're right. We can't let this trail go cold. But we don't do anything but observe when we get there, understand? We find the place, then memorize the trail back for when I have reinforcements."

He wasn't sure he could agree to her stipulation, not with his sister's life at risk. But if he didn't agree, she would dig in her heels and make it next to impossible for him to tail those men. "Understood."

She looked bone-tired briefly before her spine straightened and her chin came up to jut forward like the point of a spear. "You can track them? Then you lead."

He suspected she wanted him in front as much to keep an eye on him as to let him lead the way. He didn't care. He wasn't going to run from her.

Not yet, anyway.

"Let's pack up the tent. We may need to set up camp later." He accomplished the task quickly, and they were underway in minutes. The men hadn't covered their tracks while they were running, but about a mile from where they'd encountered the bear, they stopped blazing an obvious trail through the woods. In the dark, trying to figure out what was evidence of human passage and what was normal woodland wear and tear became a hell of a lot harder, especially with clouds scudding overhead, blocking out most of the moonlight. At least the rain had finally stopped, leaving the ground wet enough for footprints to show up in the softened soil underfoot.

"There." Three miles out, Ava spotted the faint tracks of their human prey. "Aren't those footprints?"

He studied the tracks. "Good eye," he murmured with approval.

"You're not the only tracker around here," she answered bluntly. But she sounded pleased. He spared her a quick look, struck by how pretty she was, even rain-drenched and weary. What makeup she'd been wearing back at the motel had washed away completely, leaving her looking more like the dewy-faced girl from Kentucky he'd found so fascinating when they'd met on the beach in Mariposa eight years earlier.

But looks could be deceiving. No matter how much he

might wish those intervening eight years had never happened, he couldn't deny they had. He'd changed. She'd surely changed as well.

And she was right. They weren't friends. They couldn't be.

"We need to be careful. Now that they're covering tracks, we risk running right up on them. We have to watch for an ambush."

She nodded, her expression grave. "It's not too late to go back. We can come back in daylight. Track them when the light is better."

His instincts rebelled against the idea, but he didn't trust his decision-making skills at the moment. Right now his gut was too full of fear for his sister to provide any objectivity. Tracking two well-armed men in the dark woods was clearly risky.

But was the risk worth taking?

He looked at her. "What do you think?"

She nibbled her lip again. "We keep going. By now they may realize they're missing three of their men. When those guys get back to camp, they could decide to bug out to somewhere else. If we wait until morning, we could follow this trail straight to a dead end."

He loosed a sigh of relief. "I was hoping you'd say that."

They followed the trail another hour, moving with extreme caution as the trail rose upward into the mist-veiled mountains. The climb became steeper and more treacherous, and as they neared a particularly vertical rise, Sin stopped and offered Ava a drink from a water bottle in his backpack.

She drank the water gratefully. "Don't suppose there's any way to go around that hill?"

"Not without losing at least a half hour."

She wiped her mouth with the back of her hand. "Then up we go."

"You go in front," he suggested. "You've got the bum hip. I'll be able to catch you if you lose traction."

She eyed him with caution, clearly weighing her options. No snap judgments from the Kentucky belle, he thought with a hidden smile. He'd always rather liked that about her, if he was remembering correctly.

"Okay." Turning, she reached for a handhold in the steep incline, closing her fingers around a rocky outcropping.

Sinclair stayed close behind her, distracting himself from the gnawing anxiety eating a hole in his gut by enjoying the sway of her curvy backside as she climbed the trail in front of him. She'd filled out a bit in the eight years since he'd last seen her, her once lithe, girlish body developing delightful curves in all the right places. She had the kind of hips that made a man want to sink into her and stay there forever. His hands, gripping a rough-edged rock jutting out of the hillside, itched to close around her round, firm breasts instead....

Don't get too distracted, he warned himself sternly.

The hillside started to level out, the climb less of a strain. Ava stumbled as they reached flatter ground, going down on her hands and knees. She stayed there for a moment, breathing hard.

Sinclair knelt beside her, laying his hand on her back. Her back rose and fell quickly as she caught her breath. "Sorry," she rasped.

He rubbed her back lightly. "We can take a break. How's your hip?"

She pushed herself up to a kneeling position and slid down the waistband of her pants to check the bandage. "I think it's okay."

"May I look?"

Her eyes met his, wide and wary in a shaft of pale moonlight peeking through the clouds. But she shifted, giving him better access to her injury.

Gently easing the trousers away from the bandage, he checked more thoroughly. There was a little blood seeping through the gauze, but not enough to worry. She wasn't in danger of bleeding to death.

Infection was still a major risk, however, and the longer she stayed out here in these woods without professional medical treatment, the greater the likelihood of sepsis.

He should have insisted they go back to the motel instead of chasing these men, he realized with a sinking heart. He'd been selfish and, if he was honest with himself, a little bit afraid of facing justice after so long on the run. "We should go back to the motel."

She looked at him as if he'd lost his mind. "Go back down that hill after we just climbed it? Are you kidding me?"

"The longer you and that bullet wound stay out here in these woods, the more likely you'll get an infection. That's nothing to play around with."

"I think I'm good for a few more hours." She pushed to her feet. "Let's go. We're wasting moonlight."

His heart still stuck in his throat, he rose and followed her lead.

Ten minutes later, Sin heard voices. He grabbed Ava's wrist as she continued forward, dragging her back against his chest.

She started to struggle, but he tightened his hold and whispered in her ear, "Voices."

She froze, her head coming up as if to listen.

The voices seemed to be floating toward them on the

wind, coming from somewhere dead ahead. But all Sin could see in front of them were trees, trees and more trees.

Where were the voices coming from?

"Rest a second," he whispered, letting Ava go. "I'll scout ahead. If I run into trouble, you can go for help."

Her lips pressed to a thin line. "I told you I'm not letting you out of my sight."

"Damn it, Ava—"

"I'm not letting you out of my sight," she repeated firmly. "Besides, I'm not sure I could make it back to the motel alone at this point," she added, her voice softening. "So for better or worse, we stick together."

"Stay as quiet as you can," he warned, leading the way forward. He took care with each step, moving heel to toe with deliberation, eyeing the ground ahead of them for any potential pitfalls. The voices ahead grew steadily louder, and he could make out the high, excited pitch of the conversation. Spanish, of course, but he was fluent, so he had no trouble making out the words flying about in agitation.

"How's your Spanish?" he whispered to Ava, who crept up beside him when he paused to listen.

"A little rusty," she admitted. "Haven't had a lot of chances to use it working in the Johnson City resident agency."

"It'll come back to you," he assured her. But he interpreted anyway. "Someone's taking hell for running from a bear."

"Do you recognize who's speaking?"

"Might be Cabrera," he said, uncertain. "There's a little echo. Can't be sure yet."

Suddenly, a woman's voice rang in the night, her Spanish rapid-fire but American-accented. Sin's heart clenched into a hot, hard fist.

Alicia.

"¿Dónde está mi esposo?" Fear battled with rage in her voice.

"She wants to know where her husband is," he translated for Ava.

"Yeah, I got that," she whispered grimly. "They probably killed him right off. Got rid of the extra baggage. One less captive to worry about."

Sin had never met his brother-in-law, but he hoped like hell Ava was wrong. He'd found a lot of comfort in the idea of Alicia happily married to a man she loved, a man who was good to her, who loved her and protected her when Sin couldn't.

He'd broken his sister's heart when he'd gone to Sanselmo and joined the rebels. Knowing he was a wanted man, doing things she didn't approve of for reasons she'd never understood—that kind of notoriety must have been hard for her to live with.

The last time he'd talked to her, he'd tried to explain himself, but even if he'd been able to find words to justify his actions, he couldn't tell her the whole truth, not over the phone. Maintaining his cover with *El Cambio* had been crucial to staying alive.

She'd stopped listening anyway. "I hope the next time you set a bomb, you blow yourself up," she'd told him, her voice raw with anger and pain.

Funny, he supposed, that he'd gone out and done exactly that, as far as she and the rest of the world were concerned.

As he strained to discern more of the verbal exchange between his sister and her captors, the cracking sound of a hand hitting flesh jolted through him, and Alicia's angry questions ended in a sharp cry. An answering growl rose in Sin's throat, and he rushed toward the sound of his sister's cry without thinking, stealth forgotten.

Ava's hands circled his arm and she dug her heels in, pulling him backward as he rushed forward. He tried to shake off her grip, but her fingers dug in harder, preventing him from dashing through the underbrush.

"Don't be an idiot!" she growled. "Do you want to get her killed?"

He struggled to control himself, to ease his ragged breathing and hurl cold water on his sudden rage. Ava was right. He knew she was right.

But even as he regained control of his emotions, a white-hot ball of fury festered in the center of his chest, biding its time.

Sinclair would make Cabrera and his men pay for what they'd done to his sister. He was going to find great pleasure in making sure of it.

"They're not going to do permanent damage to her, not while she's leverage," Ava whispered. He wished she sounded more confident.

"She's right there! We can get her away from them."

"Not without knowing how many people we have to take out to do it." Her voice was firmer now, her quiet competence taking some of the edge off his desperation. He grounded himself in her calm gaze, taking a few slow, deep breaths.

"Okay. Okay." He scanned the dark woods, listening to the sound of murmured conversation, trying to figure out from which direction it came. He pointed north, finally. "I think they're ahead that way. We need to get close enough to see what's what, but stay hidden."

"You were *El Cambio*. You know more about how they work than I do. How many men would Cabrera bring with him on a mission like this?"

He could only guess. Cabrera had been ruthless, unwilling to risk any sort of mutiny among his underlings.

He'd trusted few people. Sin had worked damned hard at being one of those people, and if Cabrera was here, looking for him, it was because he knew just how completely Sin had betrayed that trust.

Cabrera might be keeping Alicia alive now as leverage to get to Sin. But he didn't kid himself. Cabrera's only policy was scorched earth. There'd be no witnesses left when he was done.

"It doesn't matter how many. We have to get her away from him." The urgency of his fear forced the words from his tight throat.

"We need to get our eyes on that camp first. Know what we're up against. We need to be smart about it."

He caught her arm, tugging her around to look at him. Her eyes widened, her lips trembling apart.

The urge to kiss her, untimely and entirely out of the question, surged through him as powerfully as fear had done just a moment before. He had the ridiculous sense that if he could just kiss her, if he could feel her warm, soft body pressed to his, feel her fingers on his skin and breathe her breath into his lungs, everything would be okay.

He tore his gaze away, reminding himself that no matter what happened in the next few hours, everything would never be okay.

Ever.

He let her arm go. "Be very quiet and very careful. We'll have only one chance to get this right."

Out of the corner of his eye, he saw her check the magazine of her Glock. He reached into his pocket, pulled out one of the pistols he'd scavenged from Fuentes and Escalante and checked the magazine to see if there were any rounds left. The pistol, an FNS 9, held seventeen rounds. Fourteen remained.

He kept that one for himself and checked the other pistol. It was also an FN Herstel firearm, a twenty-round FN Five-seveN MK2. Eighteen rounds in that magazine. He offered the MK2 to Ava.

"Eighteen rounds. Use it first."

She looked up at him, her eyes suddenly widening and her lips curling inward as she nervously licked her lips.

This is her first big challenge, he realized, suddenly feeling deeply sorry for her. Despite her training, despite the FBI credentials in her pocket and the *Special Agent* in front of her name, she'd probably never been in a situation as dangerous as what they were about to face.

"If you don't want to do this, go," he said quietly. "The motel should be due west. Be careful, stay out of sight and you'll probably be there in a couple of hours. But I have to do this."

Her nostrils flared. She took the MK2 from his hands, checked the ammo herself, sighted down the barrel to familiarize herself with it and gave a short nod. "Then let's do this."

Sin felt a cracking sensation in his chest, as if something had broken open and spilled out courage and fear in equal parts. Swallowing the fear and marshaling the courage, he followed Ava forward through the woods.

CABRERA AND HIS men had set up camp in a small, sheltered cove just over the edge of a shallow escarpment. Ava had nearly stumbled over the edge of the bluff, as the trees beyond the valley camouflaged the narrow dip between ridges. She pulled up short, grabbing the trunk of a nearby pine to keep from tumbling over the edge.

Ignoring the pain in her hip and the increasing tremble of her aching thigh muscles, she dropped to her belly, seeking and finding a clearer view of the small valley that lay about twenty yards below the ridgeline.

Sin nudged his way next to her, his body warm against hers. She drew strength and determination from the solid heat of him. *Crazy,* she thought, *that I'm colluding with a terrorist to take down his buddies.*

But since she'd looked up in the parking lot of the Mountain View Lodge and seen a ghost, insanity had become the least of her problems.

From her vantage point, she could see most of the cove. There were four tents set up below. Sheltered by the low bluffs rising on either side of the encampment, Cabrera and his men showed no concern for stealth. All four of the tents were brightly lit from within, conveniently for Ava; shadows within gave her a decent head count of all the people in the camp. One in one tent, two in another, two in the third. Three men, plus Cabrera, standing in a huddle near a small campfire.

But she didn't see a woman. Had they taken her into one of the tents?

The four men moved apart, and then she saw the woman. Sinclair's sister. Small but unbowed, her spine ramrod-straight and her chin lifted, light from the campfire dancing over her delicate features. Next to Ava, Sinclair sucked in a sharp breath.

"Nine men total," she whispered. "And we dispatched three back in the woods."

"There's probably at least one more out there," he whispered back. "Cabrera has a thing about even numbers. An even dozen, plus himself. He'd like that."

"We know your sister's husband isn't down there, and she doesn't seem to know where he went. Maybe Cabrera sent one of his men off with the husband?" She didn't finish her thought—that he'd sent the henchman off to kill Gabe Cooper out of Alicia's sight.

She supposed it was merciful, at least, that they hadn't made her watch his murder. Though from what she'd heard of Cabrera's crimes, kindness and consideration weren't exactly his calling cards.

One of the men below detached from the other group, taking Alicia by the arm. Sinclair stiffened next to Ava, a low growl humming in his throat. She closed her hand over his wrist, afraid he'd launch himself over the bluff to go after his sister's captors.

"We need to go back for help. We can find this place again, can't we?" She knew the general direction they'd gone from where he'd last pitched the tent, and he surely knew how to get to the tent from the motel, since he'd found his way there and back earlier that day.

"I can't leave her there with them."

She tightened her grip on his arm, making him look at her. The look in his eyes set off a low, painful vibration somewhere in the center of her chest. "There's nothing you can do by yourself. We have to get backup, don't you see that?"

"I've seen how backup works," he said in a low, strained voice. "Backup is a damned good way to get a hostage killed."

"I can't leave you here."

"I'm getting her out of there."

She shook her head in frustration. "She thinks you're dead. Let's say you can fight your way through nine well-armed men and get to her. How easy will it be to convince her to come with you? You lied about your death. Before your death, she wished you dead. You said it yourself."

The stricken look in his eyes made her regret her words.

"I don't think she really wanted you dead," she added softly.

He took a deep, slow breath. "Okay. I'll go back with you. But I don't want the FBI involved in trying to rescue her. I remember Waco."

Not the FBI's finest moment, she had to concede. "What would you have me do, then?"

"Does Gabe Cooper's family know about the kidnapping?"

She nodded. "I'm sure they've heard by now. My partner said we'd probably be knee-deep in Coopers before we knew it."

For the first time in a while, Sinclair Solano's lips curved in a broad smile. Overhead, clouds swallowed the moon, plunging the night back into near-total darkness, but not before Ava caught a glitter of satisfaction in his midnight eyes.

"Good," he said softly, gazing down toward the cove again. "I have a feeling we'll need all the Coopers we can get."

Chapter Five

By midnight, the camp below the bluff had settled down for the night. Two men remained awake, circling the camp with AR-15 rifles strapped over their shoulders. Now and then, the burning ends of their cigarettes flared red in the darkness, narrow ribbons of smoke rising into the air overhead. Except for the occasional murmur of exchanged words between the two guards, all was silent.

Beside him, Ava carefully stretched her legs, grimacing. A whispery groan escaped her throat, barely audible. He slanted a look her way, taking in the faint sheen of perspiration on her forehead and the darkened circles under her eyes.

She was in pain, and he knew it would get worse before it got better.

Nothing was likely to happen here before morning. Even with most of the camp asleep, he and Ava were outnumbered and outgunned. The AR-15 rifles Cabrera's men carried were fitted with magazines that would hold at least thirty .223 rounds each. Almost certainly they had spare magazines in their jacket pockets. He couldn't risk thinking they didn't.

"We should find a sheltered place and set up the tent," he whispered.

Her eyes glittered at him in the dark. "And what? Get some sleep?" She shook her head.

"I need to take another look at that wound."

She dropped her hand to her hip, covering the torn fabric. "I'm okay."

He touched the back of his fingers to her forehead. Her skin was damp but hot. "You may have a fever."

"So give me an aspirin."

Pressing his lips to a thin line, he pulled a bottle of water from his pack and handed it to her. Flipping open another small pocket, he withdrew a packet of acetaminophen tablets. "Here."

She downed the pills with a couple of gulps of water. "Thanks."

"Let me deliver you back to the motel. You need medical attention."

"Deliver *me?*" She narrowed her eyes. "*You're* the prisoner."

He almost laughed but thought better of it. "At least get some sleep."

He could see in her eyes how tempting she found the idea of sleep. It would make her feel considerably better, he knew. The lack of it might hasten the deterioration of her strength.

But she thrust a belligerent chin forward. "I'm good."

Frustrated, he crept away from the edge of the bluff on all fours, rising only when he was sure he couldn't be seen from the cove below. Ava turned, propping herself on her elbows and watching him go, a look of disbelief on her face. Belatedly, she rolled over and scooted backward, mimicking his earlier movements, and finally pushed herself to her feet to face him.

"What are you doing?"

"I'm going to find a place to set up the tent and get

some sleep. Those guys down there aren't going to stay up all night to make things fair. They're getting sleep and they'll be in fighting form in the morning. Will we?"

She looked inclined to argue, but after a tense moment, she lowered her head, her shoulders slumping. He resisted the urge to brush aside the dark curls spilling over her face like a curtain, though his fingers almost ached to do so. She was tired, dirty and downright hostile, but at this moment, in the middle of his churning fear for his sister's safety, he still felt the languid tug of the sexual attraction that had sent him reeling into her path back in the sun-drenched streets of Sebastian, Mariposa.

Why? he thought. Why did it have to be Ava Trent who'd stumbled into the woods in search of him? Anyone else, he'd have ditched by now without a second thought.

Of course, anyone else might have already shot him.

He led the way back through the woods, swallowing an expletive when the heavens opened again overhead and rain started hammering through the canopy of trees. "This looks like a good spot," he muttered, unzipping his backpack. Within a couple of minutes, he'd withdrawn the tightly packed tent and Ghillie cover and set it up between a couple of sheltering mountain laurel bushes. Coaxing Ava inside, he took one last look at the tent, decided it was camouflaged enough for the dark, rainy night and crawled inside.

She had already stretched out on the tent floor, her injured side up. Her breath came in soft, labored pants, but she tried to smile as he settled down beside her. "I don't remember what it feels like to be dry."

"Get out of those wet clothes," he suggested, turning on the dim battery-powered camp lantern he'd pulled from his pack.

She arched an eyebrow in response.

"You'll warm up faster if you're not marinating in rain-soaked clothes." He waved a hand at her rain-drenched jacket and blouse.

With a sigh, she sat up and shrugged off the jacket and blouse. Beneath, her bra was black lace and satin, militantly feminine, as if her inner woman had set up a quiet rebellion against her conservative, businesslike exterior.

And under the black lace, she was all creamy curves and tempting shadows. Her stomach was flat and toned, as if she took care to keep herself in shape, but there was a voluptuous roundness to her, over the layers of muscle, that set fire to Sin's blood.

He dragged his gaze up to hers and found her staring back at him, her eyes fathomless.

"Eight years," she said as if offering an explanation.

"They've been good to you," he answered, trying to regain his equilibrium. He'd thought it impossible to think of anything but his sister's plight now that he'd seen her in captivity. Indeed, the fact that he could feel his body quickening in response to Ava's nakedness made him angry with his own weakness.

She wrapped her arms across her chest and pulled her knees up. "Do you have any extra clothes?"

He hadn't had a chance to wash anything in days, but he supposed soiled was better than wet. He found a T-shirt that didn't smell like days-old sweat and handed it to her. "I don't have any pants that will fit you."

She shrugged on the T-shirt. It was about two sizes too large for her, but her curves helped take up the extra room. Stretching gingerly, she unzipped her trousers and tried to slide them off her hips. Her face went white in the faint glow of the lantern.

He edged closer. "Let me help you."

She looked up with a soft groan. "Easy, okay?"

He took care as he helped her pull the fabric of her trousers away from the wound, willing himself to ignore the feel of her warm, firm thighs beneath his palms or the faint, sweet scent of her bath gel still clinging to her skin. He concentrated instead on her injury, noting that blood seeped through the gauze, aided, no doubt, by the rain-soaked fabric of her pants.

He hoped her clothes were wash-and-wear, because anything prone to shrinking would never survive what they'd just gone through.

"Better?" he asked once he'd pulled her legs free of the pants.

With a nod, she bit her lip and tugged the hem of the borrowed T-shirt over her hips.

"Let's change that bandage," he suggested.

She nodded again, though her brow furrowed with dread. She rolled onto her side, pulling up the hem of the T-shirt to give him a better look at the bullet graze.

It still looked terrible, all ragged, torn skin. But the wound seemed clean enough, and while the skin around the margins was a reddish-purple color, the redness hadn't yet spread much beyond the immediate area.

He talked her through the bandage change, warning her before he swabbed on stinging antiseptic and slathered the area with an antibiotic ointment. He finished off the cleaning with a fresh bandage and a new application of tape. "All done."

She tugged her knees up to her chest, keeping her eyes closed.

"You okay?" he asked.

Her head bobbed in a slight nod.

Turning away, he dug in his supplies for a change of clothes, giving her time to recover. His traveling pack was designed to be able to carry a lot of supplies in a small space, but the tent and Ghillie net took up a lot of room, even folded to their most compact states. He had little more than the clothes on his back, a second pair of jeans and three spare T-shirts, one of which Ava was currently wearing. Other things were stashed in an abandoned building in the town of Purgatory, near Quinn's new investigation agency, but it might be a long time before he'd get the chance to retrieve any of those things. If ever.

He peeled off his wet clothes and pulled out the dry jeans and one of the tees. As he was tugging on the jeans, he heard Ava suck in a sharp breath.

He turned to look at her. Her gaze was fixed on his rib cage.

On the scar.

Most days, he never gave any thought to the triptych of healed gashes that marred his rib cage. Shrapnel wounds from the explosion that had allegedly killed him. He'd cut things too close.

"Who did that to you?" Ava asked softly.

"I did it to myself," he answered just as quietly.

"Blowing something up?"

"Yes."

"You were integral to *El Cambio* for years. What changed? Why does Cabrera hate you so much now?"

He pulled the T-shirt over his head, hiding the scars. Giving himself time to figure out how much, if anything, to tell her about what he'd done to earn Cabrera's thirst for revenge. "Allegiances change."

Or they're rediscovered, he added silently.

SHE MUST HAVE SLEPT, for when she opened her eyes, it was with a start, with the jangling nerves of a person roused from slumber to an alien darkness that set her heart racing and her limbs trembling. She sat up quickly, hissing with pain as the movement sent fire racing down one side of her leg.

The ground was hard beneath her, though something with a little padding lay under her legs. Stretching her arm out to one side, she felt a flexible canvas wall. A tent, she remembered. She was in a tent.

With a dead man.

She could hear his breathing, slow and even. Damn it. She'd taken the first watch and promptly fallen asleep.

Way to go, Special Agent Trent.

Gritting her teeth against the ache in her hip, she tugged on her boots, crawled forward to the tent opening and dared a peek outside. The view through the Ghillie net was worthless, so she went a little farther, out from beneath the netting, and emerged into the cool, damp woods.

The rain had finally stopped for the night, she saw, leaving a clearing sky overhead, full of endless stars and a waxing moon dipping toward the western horizon. According to her watch, it was a little after 3:00 a.m.

She scanned the woods for any sign of movement, seeing nothing but shadows and gloom. All she heard were the normal sounds of nocturnal creatures going about their nightly activities.

It was so quiet here in the mountains. Peaceful and still. The sky above seemed endless, the stars so thick they looked like streamers of mist streaking across the midnight backdrop. The sight reminded her of a night she'd spent in Mariposa with Sinclair, lying on their backs on the roof of his rented villa watching a meteor show. A smile teased her lips, but the pleasure faded quickly as the reality of her current dilemma forced its way past the memory.

What was she going to do about Sinclair Solano? The world believed him dead, so he wasn't on anyone's radar anymore. No one's but Cabrera's, at least. Legally speaking, there was no longer a warrant out for his arrest. His face no longer graced any Wanted posters.

If she didn't tell a soul about seeing him, who would know? Or care, for that matter? For the past three years, Solano hadn't been involved in any terrorist attacks, had he?

Or had he?

A shiver wriggled down her spine, raising goose bumps on her arms and bare legs. The night was mild, typical for August in the mountains, but despite the hem of the borrowed T-shirt dipping to midthigh, she felt suddenly naked and vulnerable.

She slipped back inside the tent and ran headlong into Sinclair's chest.

His hands caught her upper arms, keeping her from toppling over. "Shh," he whispered when she opened her mouth and drew in a sharp breath.

She swallowed her cry of surprise, her body rattled by another shiver. But this reaction wasn't about the cold night air or her lingering fears.

This was all about the raspy sensation of his callused palms sliding over her bare arms, the heat of his body pressed intimately close to hers. His breath danced over her cheek, making her feel reckless and needy.

"Everything okay?" he whispered.

"Seems to be," she managed to push between her trembling lips.

He wasn't letting her go, she realized. And worse, she wasn't making any move to get away from his gentle caresses.

"You should get some sleep." His face brushed close enough to hers that she felt the light bristle of his beard against her jawline. She clenched her hands into fists, fighting the dizzying urge to rub her cheek to his, to feel the full friction of his stubble against her flesh.

He'd just said something to her, she thought numbly, trying to breathe. What had he said?

He slid his hands up her arms, over her shoulders. They came to rest on either side of her face, cradling her jaw. "Do you remember that night in Mariposa? On the roof of the villa?"

It was too dark in the tent to see much besides the inky impression of his lean, masculine features. She closed her eyes, unable to process anything more than the sensations jittering along her flesh where he touched her. "I remember."

His voice softened to a flutter of breath against her skin. "I was going to meet you the next day. I meant to, right up to the last moment."

Ice spread through her at his soft confession, and she pulled away, remembering what had happened not long after their last meeting. "But you went to Sanselmo instead." She crawled deeper into the tent, curling into a ball with her back to him.

He didn't move for a long moment, his continuing silence posing a temptation to roll over and look at him again. But she fought the urge, burying herself under eight years of anger and disappointment.

She hadn't been naive, even at the age of twenty. She'd known a man like Sinclair Solano, the idealistic son of radicals, might find freedom-fighting in a totalitarian country too tempting to resist. But even while they were soaking up the Caribbean sun, Sanselmo had been holding democratic elections for the first time in decades. They'd voted in a reformer the very day Sin had stood her up to catch a flight out of Sebastian for South America.

Why had he gone there, when what he'd claimed to be

fighting for was already starting to happen? Why had he joined a band of terrorists who, even now, continued to fight against a burgeoning civil society that had already rejected their radical aims?

Maybe he'd just been looking for a noble reason to justify his urge to kill people and blow things up. For too many people in the world, wielding destruction was motive enough for any choice they made.

His clothes rustled as he moved deeper into the tent, settling close to her. At least he didn't touch her. Her body's humiliating inability to resist his touch was something she was going to have to work through sooner or later, hopefully in the privacy of her own little apartment back in Johnson City.

"There was a man in Sebastian," he said. "My father arranged an introduction."

"Grijalva," she said quietly.

He went silent a moment, as if the word surprised him. When the silence continued, she rolled over to look at him. He sat cross-legged, his face turned toward her. In the darkness, his eyes were hidden in the shadows of his craggy forehead and aquiline nose. She could tell he was waiting for her to say more, so she added, "Luis Grijalva, the great reformer. I understand he was martyred a few months later."

Sin's lips flattened. "He was murdered. By Cabrera."

"Terrorists do have a tendency to eat their own." She knew that U.S. authorities had long suspected Grijalva's death had been staged by *El Cambio* as an attempt to discredit the new reformist government. But she was surprised to hear Sinclair admit it.

"Cabrera was the one who reported Grijalva's martyrdom. He accused Mendoza's forces of murdering Grijalva during a peaceful demonstration."

"When did you figure out he was the killer?" she asked.

"I saw it happen."

She stared at him, shocked. "You saw it?"

"It was the anniversary of the San Martín massacre. I guess you'd call it a high holy day for *El Cambio*." His brow furrowed. "Are you familiar with the San Martín massacre?"

She searched her memory. "It had something to do with Cardoso's rise to power, didn't it? A big protest that turned bloody?"

Sinclair nodded. "In the beginning, *El Cambio* was actually made up of democratic reformers trying to stop Cardoso's crackdown on free speech. Instead of the thugs who fill its ranks today, *El Cambio* started as a student movement in Sanselmo's universities. Cardoso was making even the most innocuous political speech illegal in order to maintain and expand his powers as president. The protests grew and expanded in response."

She nodded. She'd done a lot of research into the origins of *El Cambio* after learning Sinclair had joined the movement. By the time he'd signed on, the face of the rebellion had darkened considerably from its pro-democracy origins, though he hadn't seemed to realize it until too late.

"The students decided to hold a rally in San Martín, a little town in the mountains outside Tesoro. The opposition leader, Diego Montero, came to speak. They blocked the main road into the town with their protest, but the people of San Martín didn't care. It was the most excitement that had come to their little village in forever. They turned it into a festival. Until the soldiers came."

The bleak tone of Sinclair's voice set off an echo of dread in Ava's chest. She knew the gist of what had happened next.

"It was a bloodbath. Men, women, children mowed

down by Cardoso's special forces as if they were targets in a shooting gallery." Sinclair closed his eyes, horror twisting his features. "The road into town was twisty, as mountain roads are, and they had set up on a hairpin curve because the mountains made such a picturesque backdrop for the press cameras."

His words sparked a dark memory of something she'd read about the massacre. *"La Curva de los Muertos,"* she whispered, her stomach flipping.

"Dead Man's Curve," he said with a grimace. "There was nowhere to run for so many of the protestors trying to escape the gunfire. The road behind them had been blocked by the booths, and beyond the curve in the road was nothing but a rocky fifty-foot drop-off...." His voice faltered.

"And some people jumped off the cliff rather than be ripped apart by gunfire," she finished for him.

"I should have known, when Cabrera asked Grijalva to meet him there, that he had something more than talk in mind." Sinclair rubbed the furrow between his brows. "Cabrera is fond of symbolism and symmetry."

"He shot Grijalva at Dead Man's Curve?"

"He didn't shoot him. He hacked him to death with a machete."

She shuddered. "You saw it happen?"

He nodded.

"But you kept quiet?" Her voice hardened at the thought. "Your conscience its own martyr to the cause?"

There was only the tiniest of change in his expression, a flicker of movement in his lean jaw, before he answered. "*I* was the martyr."

SINCLAIR HADN'T MEANT to tell her so much of the truth. He supposed he could leave it lie, go back outside and apply himself to the job of keeping watch for what was left of the night. Let her come up with whatever explanation she wanted for his choices.

He could tell, from the horror in her expression, that whatever explanation she settled on was unlikely to be kind to him.

Maybe it would be best for both of them if she continued to see him as a murderer, a terrorist and a coward.

But when he started to move toward the front of the tent, her hand snaked out and caught his wrist. She had small, feminine hands, soft to the touch, but her grip was surprisingly strong.

"How were you a martyr?" she asked.

He thought about that day in Mariposa, when his father's urging had sent him to the beach shack where Luis Grijalva lived in exile from the nation of his birth. He had been a vigorous, fit man in his mid-fifties, old enough to present a wise face to a young man's crusade but still young enough to sway the imagination and engender passion and allegiance.

He'd spoken with passion of Sanselmo's civilized roots and the ravages two decades of totalitarian leadership had left on the land and her people. He'd talked about fairness, freedom, community and revolution, in terms so gentle it could take a while to realize he'd meant the overthrow of Sanselmo's government.

Sinclair had been young. Aimless. Trying to figure out how to stand out in a family of brilliant, passionate overachievers. Even his little sister was starting to outpace him, breezing through her studies as if they were child's play.

He'd wanted to matter.

"I went to Sanselmo because I wanted to make a difference."

"I'd say you managed that," she murmured, her voice as dry as dust.

Chapter Six

"You can imagine what life was like as the son of Martin and Lorraine Solano." Sinclair's gaze lowered to the ground in front of him. He didn't want to look at her, she realized.

Was he ashamed? She hadn't thought him capable.

"I don't think I can imagine what it's like to have famous parents." Her own parents were farmers, hardworking people who scrabbled for every extra nickel or dime to give their kids a better life. They toiled in anonymity, unknown beyond their small circle of family and friends.

But it had been a good life, even if a hard one. As far as she knew, they had no complaints, even now.

"My parents were celebrities in some political circles." Sinclair's fingers twisted around each other as they spoke. "They had expectations of the kind of lives their children would lead. I was never going to be a brilliant scholar the way Alicia was. I wasn't cut out for academia. But I wanted my life to mean something, the way theirs had."

"You thought joining a South American terrorist group would give your life meaning?" She tried not to sound so harsh, but she had trouble understanding how he could have been so shortsighted. Even at twenty, she'd been able to figure out that a group of heavily-armed rebels wanting to thwart a reform movement already underway couldn't be up to any good.

Why hadn't he seen it?

"I thought *El Cambio* wanted a democratic revolution."

"So did a lot of people. But the Mendoza government was making changes already—"

He shot her a sharp look. "*El Cambio* believed Mendoza was just a puppet for the old Cardoso regime."

"Guess we'll never know, since *El Cambio* killed Mendoza before he could institute all his proposed reforms."

He held her gaze for a long moment, then looked back at his hands again. "Wouldn't have mattered. *El Cambio* wanted the power for themselves. And they were willing to break any rule, all rules, to get it."

"Took you eight months to figure that out?"

"I saw what I wanted to believe and ignored the rest. Chalked it up to the brutality of the regime, goading people into acting in ways they wouldn't otherwise."

"The regime had already changed by the time you went to Sanselmo," she pointed out gently. "Mendoza was cleaning up the government, purging the brutes out of the military. Civil society was forming on its own, without the help of the rebels."

"We wanted everything immediately."

"Because that ever happens."

He shot her an angry look. "People are always promised change when it's time to mark the ballot. But it so rarely happens when the counting is over. The people of Sanselmo had lived with their necks under the boot for too many years."

"I know."

"How?" he asked, sounding curious. "You seem to know a hell of a lot about a South American country most Americans probably couldn't point out on a map."

"I made it my business to find out all about what was going on in Sanselmo," she admitted. "Once I figured out that was where you were headed."

"How *did* you know that was where I was headed?"

"I was already thinking about becoming an investigator by the time we met. I had…instincts for it." And, if she could admit it to herself, at least, she wanted to know just what her holiday fling was about to get himself into.

"Did you follow me?"

"Not exactly." She stretched her legs out in front of her before realizing there wasn't really much room for stretching inside the small tent. She tugged her knees back up to her body. "I followed your trail. Learned you'd talked to a man the locals called *El Pavón.* The peacock."

"*El Pavón?* Hmm." He seemed to give the name some thought. "I suppose, in retrospect, it fit."

From what little she'd been able to see of Luis Grijalva, she concurred. She'd glimpsed him, briefly, in one of the open-market cafés in the Mariposa capital. A trim, compact man with a well-groomed mane of graying hair and a neat mustache and goatee, he'd been a striking figure in his bright island colors and regal bearing.

Even with her inbred skepticism of people who claimed to be revolutionaries, she'd found him charismatic and appealing.

How much more would Sinclair, fed the mother's milk of revolutionary idealism at his parents' feet, have been susceptible to Grijalva's sway? He'd already admitted he'd been looking for meaning in his life.

Grijalva must have seen an easy mark in Sinclair Solano.

"What did you do when you found out I'd talked to Luis Grijalva?" he asked.

Her lips quirked again. "Threw up my hands, called you a fool and hopped the next plane back to the States."

No need to tell him that she'd cried the whole plane trip home.

He shifted restlessly. "You haven't asked the obvious question yet."

She released a long, slow breath. "What question is that?"

He lifted his gaze to meet hers. "Why, if I had figured out what *El Cambio* was all about eight months into my association with them, did I stick around the group for another four years?"

It was an excellent question, but she wasn't sure she wanted to know the answer. Life had been much neater when she'd been able to tuck her memories of Sinclair Solano in a little box she could shove into the back of her mental closet, never to be reexamined. Easier to say, "He was some guy I met on vacation. I hardly even remember him."

Much harder to sit in front of him, his body close enough to send undulating waves of heat washing over her. Close enough to notice, once again, how ridiculously long and dark his eyelashes were, or how his lean features made him almost as beautiful as he was handsome.

"Okay," she said quietly, "I'll bite. Why did you stay with *El Cambio* after you knew what they were?"

His dark eyes held hers, full of secrets and mysteries. But as he opened his mouth, drew in a long slow breath in preparation to speak, something snapped outside the tent.

He whirled to face the entrance, the muscles of his back bunched in anticipation of whatever happened next. He was lean but strong, his body thicker and more toned than it had been when she'd known him before. Life since their interlude in Mariposa had hardened him. Given what he'd been doing for many of those years, she supposed it was no surprise.

He'd trained with terrorists. Hiked through unforgiving jungles and climbed volcanic peaks in the rainforest lair of *El Cambio.* And there was no telling what he'd been doing in the past few years, when the world had thought him dead and gone.

"Stay here," he whispered.

"No," she whispered back, crawling behind him to the tent door.

The Ghillie net extended about five feet past the front of the tent. Sinclair paused under the Ghillie net, peering out into the darkness of the woods beyond. Rain had started falling again, but lightly now, barely seeping through the netting to drip down the back of Ava's neck as she hunched closer to Sinclair. He edged over, making room for her, and peered through the netting, trying to see what may have made the loud cracking noise outside the tent.

Mist rose around them, turning the woods into an ethereal realm of dark shadows and ghostly tendrils of moisture. Staying very still, she peered into the gloom, trying to soften the focus of her gaze so that she'd be better able to spot any sign of movement outside.

But there was nothing. No movement. No sounds.

Sin's hand closed around her elbow, nudging her back toward the tent. She slipped inside, watching as he crawled through behind her.

"Could have been an animal," he said quietly.

She nodded, clenching her jaws against a sudden tremor that rolled through her like an ocean wave.

"We're probably not going to get many better chances to get some sleep," he whispered.

"I don't think I can sleep."

"I don't think you can afford not to."

She knew he was right, but the thought of closing her eyes and relaxing her guard went against all her instincts. Especially when she'd be trusting her life to a man whom, twenty-four hours ago, she'd have called a traitor without a second thought.

"Why did you stay with *El Cambio?*" she asked after a few moments of tense silence.

He didn't answer. She peered through the dark, trying to see his face, but he had settled with his back to her. If he'd heard her question, he clearly didn't intend to answer.

She curled up in a tight knot, wishing she were back at the Mountain View Motor Lodge, tucked into a warm, dry bed. She wished she'd never looked across the parking lot and seen the face of a ghost. She wished someone else had been in the office when the missing-persons call came in from the Poe Creek locals.

In short, she wished she were anywhere but stuck here in a damp tent with Sinclair Solano, the only man she'd never been able to forget—or forgive.

SIN WASN'T SURE why he hadn't answered her whispered question. Only a few minutes before, he'd been on the verge of telling her everything, after all. If they hadn't heard the twig snap, he might have already spilled all the details. So why hadn't he answered when she asked him again?

"Nobody will ever believe your story," Alexander Quinn had warned him when he'd finally come in from the cold. "They'll think you're making excuses for your actions. And the CIA won't be able to back you up. We don't discuss undercover missions that way, especially when we still have ongoing operations in the arena."

Sinclair had accepted the fact that he'd still be living a lie. He'd thought, at the time, it was worth it. It wasn't like he could go back home to his family. His parents had been as blind about *El Cambio* as he had been, and they'd hardly be proud of knowing how he'd worked for the CIA to bring the terrorist group to its knees.

His sister hated him. She'd wished him dead shortly before he'd faked his own demise, and he didn't suppose she'd changed her mind since. Even now, putting his life on the line to rescue her, he doubted she'd be happy to see him. But he'd figured separation from his family was part of the price he'd paid for his mistakes.

Besides, the truth was such a cliché. Disillusioned radical agrees to turn double agent for the CIA.

Who would buy a story like that?

ALEXANDER QUINN TIGHTENED the straps of his backpack and plodded, head down, toward the motel parking lot a quarter mile down the road. He'd dressed for the weather—heavy rain slicker over sturdy jeans and a long-sleeved T-shirt—and his hiking boots were weatherproof by design. To anyone who bothered to notice him, he looked like any of the thousands of hikers who followed the Appalachian Trail during the hiking season, though he was miles west of the trail itself.

A large blue SUV moved past him, headlights slicing through the rainy gloom, and turned into the parking lot of the Mountain View Motor Lodge. The plates, he noted, were local, but a large sticker from a rental car agency covered part of the bumper.

He slowed his pace as he neared the parking lot, keeping an eye on the SUV. He'd been expecting Coopers to converge on the motel ever since he'd seen the first report of the missing tourists. He had a feeling they'd finally arrived.

Six people emerged from the SUV, dark silhouettes in

the pools of golden light spilling from the tall lamps illuminating the motel's parking lot. Four men, two women. As he edged closer, another SUV passed him and pulled into the parking lot, lining up next to the other vehicle. Four more people emerged from the second SUV, three men, one woman.

Quinn paused on the shallow shoulder across the road, watching as the ten new arrivals huddled together in muddy yellow light from the parking lot lamps. He recognized all of them, though he'd had only minimal dealings with most. The occupants of the first SUV were mostly Gabe Cooper's siblings—brothers, J.D., Jake and Luke; sister, Hannah; Hannah's husband, Riley; and J.D.'s wife, Natalie. The second vehicle's occupants were Gabe's cousins, Jesse, Rick and Isabel, plus Isabel's husband, Ben Scanlon.

All experienced trackers, Quinn thought. Good. They'd need all the skills they could muster.

One of the Coopers turned his head suddenly, his gaze locking with Quinn's before he could look away. Jesse Cooper. The other man's eyebrows lifted slightly, but he looked away deliberately, as if ignoring Quinn's presence.

He waited as the Coopers and their various spouses moved around the crime-scene tape and headed for the small motel office located at the far end of the parking lot.

One of them peeled away from the others and started walking toward the edge of the parking lot across from where Quinn stood watching. Not Jesse Cooper, as he might have expected, but Jake Cooper. Gabe's twin.

Jake stood at the edge of the road, staring across the narrow two-lane, as if daring Quinn to make the next move.

He was tempted to turn and walk away. Let the Coopers fend for themselves. They were big boys and girls.

They'd handled tough situations in the past, and Quinn knew they could cope without his help if necessary.

But he had his own reasons for sticking his nose in this missing-persons investigation. He had his own missing person to find.

He crossed the road at a leisurely pace, not making direct eye contact with Jake. He stopped when he reached the parking lot, standing several feet away from the other man. The rain that had been a deluge earlier in the evening had reemerged as a drizzle, generating a ghostly mist that settled across the valley like a gossamer shroud. Though Jake Cooper stood only a few feet away, he looked almost spectral in the swirling fog.

"Do you know who has them?" Jake asked in a conversational tone.

"I have a theory," Quinn answered in a similar tone.

"Care to share it?"

"I don't think it's about your brother. I think it's about Alicia."

Jake's eyes narrowed. "Is it Cooper Security related, then?"

Quinn shook his head no. "It goes back further than that."

"Is it related to Hamilton Gray?"

Quinn hadn't even thought about Gray, the serial killer Alicia had helped capture and convict. "As far as I know, he's still in prison, exhausting all his appeals."

"Then what?" Jake's voice tightened with impatience. "Do you even remember how to hold a straightforward conversation?"

"Alicia had a brother."

Jake stared across the misty void between them. "Her brother's dead."

"Is he?" Quinn started walking away.

"You're a cryptic son of a bitch!" Jake called after him.

Quinn kept walking, unable to argue.

THE BOMB WAS unsophisticated but powerful. ANFO—Ammonium nitrite and fuel oil—easy to procure, easy to use. Some of the *El Cambio* crew had wanted to emulate their counterparts on the other side of the world and use more technologically sophisticated improvised explosive devices, but for sheer destructive force, ANFO worked nicely.

Despite his reputation with the FBI and other American law-enforcement agencies, Sinclair wasn't a bomb maker. There were really only a handful of *El Cambio* operatives who dealt with explosives on a regular basis, but Cabrera and his lieutenants found value in cultivating the idea that all members of *El Cambio* were equally skilled and lethal.

He also liked to make sure that everyone in the group had blood on their hands. Sinclair had been fortunate, to that point, that his skills as an artist and propagandist had kept him out of the real dirty work.

But that day, his time of reckoning had come.

"It's a simple timer," Cabrera had explained as he'd handed Sin the keys to the panel van. "All you have to do is park the truck in front of the warehouse, set the timer for twenty minutes and walk away."

An easy task. And an impossible one.

He hadn't contacted Alexander Quinn in two months. The spy had seemed surprised to hear from him.

"You're blowing up what?" Quinn had asked.

"I'm not blowing up anything," Sin had answered bluntly. "How do I get out of this?"

"You don't," Quinn said. Then he'd rattled off directions that had made Sinclair's head spin.

But he'd followed them to the letter. And at the end of the day, he'd had blood on his hands. Including his own.

But no innocents had died that day.

In the pale gray light seeping through the narrow tent opening, Sinclair looked at the tight white burn scar on the inside of his forearm. It disappeared under the sleeve of his T-shirt, but the puckered flesh extended all the way up his arm. He'd cut things too close that day in Tesoro. Waffled over his choices a little too long.

Nine men had died in the explosion, all *El Cambio* rebels.

Sinclair Solano should have been victim ten, as far as the rest of the world had known. The explosion had blown several of the bodies out into the harbor, including the borrowed body from the morgue. Most of the bodies had been recovered, or at least parts of them had. Enough for a body count. Sinclair himself had gone into the harbor, his shrapnel wounds shrieking with agony as he swam through the burning debris to the rendezvous point he and Quinn had agreed upon.

Quinn had almost given up on him by the time he dragged himself onto the rocks and into his spy handler's strong grasp. The next few hours had been a blur, alternating waves of agony and painkillers. Quinn, meanwhile, had made sure the Sanselmo authorities had a copy of his DNA to make the identification on the unidentified body they pulled from the harbor. Nobody had to know that the DNA actually belonged to the homeless dead man Quinn had procured from the local morgue.

As far as the world was concerned, Sinclair Solano had died that day in Tesoro Harbor. And he'd stayed dead for three and a half long, lonely years.

So how had Cabrera figured out he was still alive?

"What time is it?" Ava Trent's sleepy voice seeped

through his skin into his bones, setting them humming. He looked up to find her propped on her elbows, watching him through a mass of brown, humidity-frizzed hair. She looked tired and a little pale, but he found her tempting anyway. And as much as he'd like to pretend it was situational—three years without sex could make any man crazy—deep down he knew there was something fundamentally different about the way Ava Trent made him feel.

It had been that way eight years ago as well. On an island full of exotic beauties, it had been the fresh-faced, no-nonsense Kentucky farm girl who'd managed to turn him inside out.

He realized she was waiting for an answer, and it took a second to remember what she'd asked. He checked his watch. "Just before six."

"Don't suppose you have any food stashed away in that bag of yours?"

He had a couple of protein bars, but he'd meant to replenish his supplies days ago. He should have gone into town sooner. But he'd thought he had time. What was the rush? He had nowhere to go.

Until he'd heard the news about his sister and her husband going missing.

He opened his pack and tossed her one of the protein bars. "Make it last. There's only one more."

She ripped open the packaging and took a bite, a low moan escaping her throat. He dragged his gaze away, tamping down the arousal throbbing in his veins. He concentrated on the contents of his backpack, noting with alarm that his supplies were rapidly dwindling.

"You ever going to tell me why you stayed with *El Cambio* so long after you knew what they were up to?"

He looked at her, once more tempted to spill everything. But her jaw was set, her eyes sharp with skepticism, and he just wasn't in the mood for her to shoot down the truth again. "Not much point, since you won't believe me."

She shrugged as if it didn't matter, but he could tell she wasn't quite as nonchalant as she wanted to appear. Maybe, sooner or later, she'd be willing to listen.

And maybe he'd be willing to talk. "How soon do you think we can get going?" she asked around another bite of the protein bar.

"As soon as possible," he answered resolutely, zipping his bag. "We need to get back to civilization."

She handed him the remaining half of the protein bar and stretched her limbs, wincing as the motion pulled against her healing wound. Muscles bunched and twitched her jaws, but she managed not to groan, even though Sin could tell she was in pain.

"Maybe you should stay here and rest," he suggested, finishing off the protein bar in a couple of bites. The little bit of food took the edge off his hunger but didn't banish it. He needed real food. A real bath. A real bed.

But not until he got his sister back.

"You're my prisoner, remember?" she asked, grimacing as she pushed herself to a crouch. "You go nowhere without me."

"Right." He exited through the tent and peered through the Ghillie net, surveying the mist-shrouded woods around them. Everything looked quiet at the moment.

But he knew that situation could change in a heartbeat.

Chapter Seven

The morning was cool, the air misty, as Ava trudged through the woods behind Sinclair. They were still in the middle of sunrise, the sky peeking through the dense trees overhead a rosy pink starting to give way at the edges to a clear, pale blue. The sun remained behind the crest of the mountains to the east, but there was enough light to make them vulnerable if anyone was out there in the woods looking for them, so they moved ahead at a slow, steady pace.

At least, Ava told herself that was why Sinclair was moving so slowly. Because the alternative was admitting that her wounded hip and the previous day's exertions had left her hobbled like an arthritic woman three times her age. She was not ready to face such an embarrassing notion.

They were moving steadily west toward Poe Creek, though the path they took was anything but straight. They stayed close to the trees, moving with as much stealth as they could manage. So far, they'd spotted no sign of Cabrera's men in the woods.

But Ava could feel them nearby, like a poisonous miasma hovering just over the horizon, gathering strength and malignance.

"Need to stop and catch your breath?" Sin paused

behind the trunk of a large fir tree and pulled a water bottle from his backpack. He took a long drink and handed the open bottle to her.

She took a drink. The water was tepid but felt cool and satisfying going down. She handed the bottle back and peered around for any sign of movement. "Do you think they've given up looking for us?"

He shook his head. "I'm not sure they've ever been looking for us, exactly."

"Surely one of those men we've taken out had time to radio back to camp."

"I didn't find any radios on them."

"Then they used cell phones. Or satellite phones. We didn't stop and search them carefully." She grimaced at the flash of pain that shot through her wounded hip. "Maybe we should have."

"We were running for our lives," he said bluntly, stashing the water in his pack. "You need a little longer?"

She squared her shoulders. "No, let's keep moving."

They couldn't have been more than a mile or so from the highway that wound past the Mountain View Motor Lodge, but they were still trudging a winding path through the woods, a long way from anything approaching civilization, nearly an hour later.

The sun was over the mountains by then, angling through the trees in lambent beams that reflected off the low-lying mist. The effect was ethereal, like walking through a golden fog, and if Ava hadn't been so tense and tired, she might have enjoyed the experience.

But all she wanted right now was to reach civilization, where she had options. Last night, she and Sinclair had agreed that setting the FBI on Cabrera's gang might not be the smartest way to go, but daylight had a sobering effect, reminding her that for all the well-documented weaknesses in the organization she called home, the FBI was still well-equipped to deal with ruthless terrorists.

"So are the Coopers," Sinclair said flatly a few minutes later when she voiced her change of heart. "And they have a vested interest in getting Alicia out of there alive, unlike the FBI."

"The FBI isn't in the habit of sacrificing civilians, you know."

He shot a hard, skeptical look her way. "Their track record might suggest otherwise."

"You can't hold a couple of high-profile failures against them. They have a long record of good work."

"You have an institutional loyalty to the Bureau that I don't have."

She wasn't going to win this argument, so she changed tacks. "How do you know the Coopers have even arrived yet?"

"Because that's what the Coopers do." He pulled up short, forcing Ava to stutter-step to a halt to keep from slamming into his back. His shoulders went tense, his head lifting.

"What?" she whispered as he remained utterly still.

"I thought I heard something in the woods ahead." He turned to glance back at her. "Could have been an animal."

Could have been a terrorist, she countered silently. She saw a similar unspoken thought glittering behind his dark eyes.

She pulled the MK2 pistol he'd given her the night before from its hiding place in her waistband. "Charge or retreat?"

He took a second to think about it. "Retreat. We could be outnumbered."

And would continue to be outnumbered, she thought

grimly, until they reached civilization and could call in reinforcements.

"What will your partner do when you don't show up for breakfast?" Sin asked a moment later, as they started backtracking toward another westward trail out of the woods.

She wasn't sure he'd even notice. But she supposed protocol would demand that Landry call in her disappearance, even if he thought she might have a good reason for being away from the motel.

"He'll call it in, I guess."

"How soon?"

She glanced at his watch. Almost eight. "I figure we have at least an hour. He's not going to start looking for me before nine."

"It would be better if we could prevent the FBI from swooping in here and causing havoc," he said quietly, as if they hadn't had almost this very argument a few minutes earlier.

"How are we supposed to find the Coopers?" she asked.

"They'll be at the motel. They've probably already rousted your partner out of bed, as a matter of fact," Sin said with a grimace. "Which might mean that extra hour is as good as gone."

"I thought they liked to do things their own way, without official interference," she said.

Sinclair considered the thought. "Maybe. Maybe they'll try to go around your partner. Is he the sort who can be played that way?"

She didn't like to admit it, but Landry's apathy probably made him the perfect FBI agent for the Coopers to deal with. He wouldn't ask too many complicated questions, and he wasn't going to go the extra mile to find out what was really going on behind the scenes of this kidnapping, or even her own disappearance.

She wondered what had happened to Landry to make him such a dead-ender. When he'd first been assigned to the Johnson City office, she'd made a point of looking at his jacket to see what kind of FBI agent he'd been in his last few assignments.

On paper, he'd looked good. Commendations, a good solve rate, plenty of kind words from superiors and peers alike. But at some point between his last big case in the Richmond field office and his reassignment to the Johnson City resident agency, things had changed for Cade Landry.

Maybe, if she and Sinclair got out of this mess alive, she'd make the effort to find out what had happened to Landry. But her case partner's history was so far down her list of things to worry about at the moment, she shoved all thoughts of him aside.

"They'll be able to go around him if that's their intention," she answered Sinclair's earlier question. "Which brings up the next question—if the Coopers are here in Tennessee and are caught up on what's going on, what's their next move?"

Sinclair seemed to give the question some thought as he pushed ahead through the dense underbrush. He moved with fluid grace, she noted as she struggled to emulate his easy gait. He'd had some experience moving silently and maintaining a low profile, obviously.

He'd managed to stay off everyone's radar for three years, after all. The official government assessment had been that he'd died in the harbor explosion three years ago, and nothing had come across her desk to suggest the official assessment was wrong.

Yet, here he was, very much not dead.

She was relieved when he stopped for another rest about twenty minutes later, hunkering down beside her on a fallen tree trunk sheltered from the rest of the woods by a dense stand of young Fraser firs. He offered her a drink of water first, and she took a couple of swigs gratefully, wondering why they weren't any closer to the road after so much trekking through the woods.

"Are we going in circles?" she asked as she handed back the water bottle.

"We did for a bit," he answered, taking one quick drink of water before returning the half-empty bottle to his backpack. "I thought we should take precautions, in case someone is tracking us."

The hair on the back of her neck prickled. "You think that's happening?"

"I think we shouldn't take a lot of chances," he answered after a brief pause. "If any of those men in the woods had a chance to tell Cabrera what was going on before we stopped them, then he knows his plan to kidnap Alicia to smoke me out is working."

"How does he know you're alive? As far as I know, nobody else has a clue you're not fish food in the middle of Tesoro Harbor."

He grimaced at her description. "I don't know."

"Does anyone else know you're alive?"

She could see his thoughts swirling behind his dark eyes. After a moment, he nodded. "At least two people. One I trust completely. One I think I can probably trust, but—"

"But you can't be sure?"

"It would take only a word to the wrong person. A slip of the tongue." He looked as if he wanted to say more, but he stopped, pressing his mouth to a thin line.

"Who's the one you trust?"

She thought for a moment he wasn't going to answer her question. Then he released a quiet sigh and said, "He's a former CIA agent."

She tried not to look skeptical, but the expression in his eyes made it clear she'd failed.

"I know it sounds like a bad movie," he said with another quiet huff of breath. "But it's true. When I lost faith in what *El Cambio* was doing, I turned myself in at the American consulate in Tesoro. The CIA agent was the first person I talked to."

"And he, what? Offered you a chance to go back inside *El Cambio* as a double agent?" she said with a soft laugh.

His lips flattened further. "I told you it sounded like a bad movie."

She stared at him, realizing her outlandish guess was the story he was apparently going with. "Come on."

"It's the truth."

She didn't know what to say. He seemed earnest enough, but she was in no position to believe everything he had to say.

"Forget it," he said after a few seconds. "It's not that important. All you need to know is that this guy I know can help us if I can reach him."

"How do you know he's not the one who betrayed you to Cabrera?"

"Because he put his neck on the line to get me out of Sanselmo safely and set me up with a new identity."

"What new identity?"

"Christopher Peralta. Although I suppose it doesn't really matter anymore. Chris Peralta's been compromised, too." He nodded toward the west. "We need to be on the move."

Her legs were beginning to ache in concert with her bullet wound in protest of so much trudging around through underbrush, but she gritted her teeth and did her best to keep pace with Sinclair.

Somewhere around midmorning, they reached the section of the woods where Ava had run into the ambush the day before. She didn't recognize it, and the bodies of the dead terrorists no longer lay where they'd left them, but Sinclair assured her they'd arrived back in the same place. "I've spent the past year wandering these woods and mountains," he told her as he crouched next to a mountain laurel bush that looked as if it had been shorn in half, several branches now lying broken and flat on the ground. "This is where Escalante's body fell."

"So their compadres retrieved the bodies?"

"They don't want to risk announcing their presence here until they're ready to strike,"

She looked around, trying to picture the place as she remembered it. But everything had happened so fast, including Sinclair's hauling her off to the safety of his tent. She could barely remember the details of the ambush itself, much less where it had happened.

"They're out here looking for us. You know that, right?"

She nodded, trying to ignore the gooseflesh that scattered down her arms in response to his warning. "I know that."

"Then we shouldn't linger." He started walking again.

She trudged behind him, the skin on the back of her neck still crawling.

BY NOON, THE temperature had risen to the mid-eighties, and the lingering moisture from the previous night's storms made the woods feel like a sauna. If he'd been alone, Sinclair might have skipped lunch and kept going, but Ava was running on sheer, dogged determination and not much else. "We stop here," he announced, pulling the Ghillie net from his backpack.

She stared at the camouflage net. "We're not going to set up the tent, are we?"

He wondered if she knew how much longing he could hear in her voice when she asked that question. "No, but I figured we'd take a longer rest and eat the other protein bar. Rehydrate. Might as well camouflage ourselves while we're doing it."

While he draped the Ghillie net across several shrubs, giving them a small shelter for their midday rest, she dug in his backpack and pulled out the last protein bar and a bottle of water. "Are there any creeks around here clean enough to risk refilling our water bottles?"

"Yeah, though I'd still rather boil it first. And we're fresh out of fires." He sat down next to a patch of mossy ground and patted the spot beside him. "Sit. Take a nap if you want. It's too hot out there for hiking right now, but if you wait around, we're bound to get an afternoon shower or two. Cool things right off."

"Oh, goody. More rain." But she settled on the patch of moss beside him and tore the paper off the protein bar.

"You'll be glad for the drop in temperature."

"I know." She straightened the grimace from her face and managed a half smile as she broke the protein bar in half and gave him his portion. She ate her half slowly, though she had to be hungry by now. He pressed the water on her as well, not liking her pallor or the rapid rate of her breathing. It would be very easy to fall victim to dehydration and heat exhaustion, especially for a woman who was already injured.

He managed to get half the bottle of water down her before her eyelids began to droop. Edging closer, he let her lean against him, her head wobbling before it finally dropped against his shoulder.

A fluttery feeling settled in the center of his chest, reminding him of a time that seemed a lifetime distant, a time when he'd been a young man on the cusp of his wide-open future. A time when a hazel-eyed girl from Nowhere, Kentucky, had stolen his breath and shown him a whole world of possibilities he'd never considered before.

What if he'd met her that night in Mariposa rather than tracking down Luis Grijalva? Where would he be right now?

Not here, he thought. Not hiding in the woods from Alberto Cabrera. Not wondering how much longer Ava Trent could keep walking before her weariness and injury overcame her gritty willpower.

But would *El Cambio* be on the run the way it was now? Would Sanselmo be so close to stability and economic promise if he hadn't taken up Alexander Quinn's offer to turn double agent? So much of the information he'd fed to the CIA had helped defang *El Cambio.* He'd helped put some of the more brutal drug cartels on the run, as well.

Would he really be willing to turn his back on the good things he'd done, no matter how mistaken his choices in the beginning?

God, he needed to talk to Quinn. The man might be as slippery as an eel in slime, but he had a way of getting to the bottom line of any question.

He'd know what to do next.

ALEXANDER QUINN WASN'T a man who liked to sit around and wait for things to happen, even though, technically, his job with the CIA had been all about waiting for things to happen, things he'd set into motion himself. He'd done what he could to put the Cooper family into motion the night before, but so far, they were still holed up in the motel across the road, waiting for God only knew what.

More Coopers to arrive? Not a bad idea, given what Quinn suspected was going on out in those woods.

He was pretty sure Sinclair Solano was still somewhere

in this general area. That fact, combined with the abduction of his sister, could be no coincidence. Someone was clearly trying to use Alicia Cooper to draw her brother into the open.

But who? Who knew Solano was still alive?

Kidnapping a security agent and her tough, physically fit husband from their motel room had been a brazen act. It hadn't been accomplished easily. It had taken planning, and certainly required more than a single perpetrator. Quinn had put out some feelers to his former colleagues at the company, but he'd heard nothing of any interest so far.

He wasn't surprised, exactly, by the lack of response. His recent decision to leave the CIA for private work had caught everyone by surprise. He supposed everyone in the agency had expected him to die somewhere in the bowels of Langley and be entombed there without ceremony, just another gold star on the anonymous wall of honor.

Himself included.

His cell phone hummed lightly against his hip. He reached into his pocket, studied the unlisted number and considered not answering.

But curiosity overcame caution. "Yeah?"

"Did you know the Mountain View Motor Lodge rooms have back exits?" The voice on the other end of the phone belonged to Jake Cooper.

The hair on the back of Quinn's neck prickled. "Where are you?"

"In the woods about a quarter mile from where you're standing."

"How'd you get this phone number?"

"We have friends in your agency."

Probably Sutton Calhoun, Quinn thought. Calhoun had worked for Cooper Security before taking the job with Quinn. Could have been Adam Brand, too, he supposed—Brand had been close with Isabel Cooper and her husband, Ben Scanlon.

Conflicting loyalties could be very messy indeed.

"Who's with you?" he asked Jake.

"Luke, Hannah, Riley, Jesse and Rick. Everybody else has set up a clearinghouse for information at the motel. We have agents following a lot of potential leads."

"What are the six of you planning to do?"

"Local law enforcement officers had reports of gunshots heard in the woods just east of here yesterday afternoon. It's not hunting season."

Quinn bit back a curse. He hadn't even thought to check in with the local LEOs. One of the downsides of playing the lone wolf, he supposed.

"Why are you calling me?" he asked.

There was a brief pause on the other end of the call. Then Jake said quietly, "We need some information. Did you know that one of the FBI agents who came to town yesterday to help the locals investigate has gone missing?"

A ripple of surprise raced down Quinn's back. "For how long?"

"She disappeared soon after she and her associate arrived. Isabel worked a case with the partner, Cade Landry, a couple of years ago. She ran into him this morning. Apparently the missing agent never came to pick up the room key he got for her, wasn't in her room when he tried to check in with her this morning, and there's no sign she stayed there at all last night."

Disturbing, Quinn thought. "What do we know about the missing agent?"

"Ava Trent. Female. Twenty-eight. Brown hair, hazel eyes. Works out of the Johnson City resident agency. About six years with the Bureau."

"Any sign of foul play?"

"No. Landry said she wandered toward the woods yesterday afternoon after telling him to get them a couple of rooms. Last he saw of her."

Wandered toward the woods, Quinn thought, his eyes narrowing as he turned and looked at the deepening woods behind him.

"We're going to see if we can find any sign of her." Jake's voice broke into Quinn's queasy thoughts. "Want to come along?"

Another downside of getting in the habit of going it alone, Quinn thought. It had never occurred to him to join forces with the Coopers.

It should have.

"What's your exact location?" he asked.

Jake rattled off longitude and latitude numbers. "I assume you have a GPS locator at your disposal?"

"Of course."

"We'll wait fifteen minutes for you to find us. Be here or we leave without you."

Quinn had already started heading in the general direction of the coordinates Jake had given him. "And then what?"

"And then, we go find my brother and Alicia."

"You don't know what you're up against."

"Do you? Does this have something to do with Alicia's brother's activities in South America?"

Quinn couldn't answer. But apparently his silence was enough.

"If he's still alive, there are people who would want their hands on him," Jake murmured, his voice barely audible over the phone. "And they'd have no problem using Alicia as a pawn, would they?"

"If he were still alive, and they thought they could use

her to smoke him out of hiding, no. No, they'd have no problem with that at all."

Jake Cooper muttered a profanity. "Twelve minutes now. Get a move on." He hung up the phone.

Quinn shoved his phone in his pocket and quickened his pace. It might go against his long-ingrained habits to be a team player, but maybe it was time to form some new habits.

Right now, he had a feeling he could use all the help he could get.

Chapter Eight

Ava opened her eyes to a gloomy half twilight. It took a second to gather her wits enough to realize she was napping against a warm, solid body underneath the ruffled camouflage of a Ghillie net.

She sat upright and rubbed her gritty eyes. "How long did I sleep?" she whispered.

"About two hours." Sinclair's quiet voice rumbled through her from the point where their bodies touched, flooding her with instant heat.

She looked at Sinclair, dismayed by how long she'd delayed their escape. "That's too long."

"You needed it." He brushed a tousled hank of hair away from her eyes. His fingertips lingered against the curve of her cheek, setting her skin on fire. "You look better for it."

She tried to drag her gaze away from his, but the light caress of his fingertips on her face seemed to trap her in place. "Sinclair—"

"I never thought I'd see you again. But I thought of you so many times over the years." He spoke as if reluctant, as if begrudging each word that slipped between his lips. But his dark eyes blazed with a pulsating hunger that set off an answering throb low in her belly. "I didn't want to. I wanted to put everything in my former life behind me.

I knew what I was committing to, and I knew I couldn't go back once I made the choice."

"Why?" she whispered. "Why did you choose *El Cambio?* Sanselmo was already beginning to reform the government. If you'd just given them a little more time—"

His thumb brushed over her lower lip. "I was young and impatient. And I had a head full of foolish ideas about the way the world should be."

"Everybody does." She tried to ignore the way his gaze dropped to her lips, but she was powerless against the surge of longing that rose in her chest to strangle her. "You think I didn't have things I wanted to change?"

"You were smart enough to take things slowly." A mournful note darkened his voice. "I had my mother's ideas in my head and my father's passion in my breast. And Luis Grijalva's revolutionary words in my ears. I thought there was no other choice to be made. I wanted to make a difference, and joining the revolution was the only way I could do it."

She could see in his pain-filled gaze how much he regretted his choices. "How many people did you kill for your passion?" she asked, because she needed to remind herself of the monster he'd become, not the foolish boy he'd once been.

"I killed nine people in that last bomb blast," he answered. "I didn't mean to, but they rushed the warehouse early. I tried to time it so that my hands would remain clean, but—" He dropped his hand away from her face.

"You mean the only people you killed that whole time you were with *El Cambio* were your fellow terrorists?"

"I was never a bomber," he said flatly, his fists clenching at his sides.

"But the indictments against you—"

"The government got me mixed up with another rebel,"

he said quietly, his gaze dropping to the ground between them. "My CIA handlers let the mistake remain. It gave me more cachet with *El Cambio,* being one of the FBI's most wanted."

Could he be telling the truth? Or were these more convenient lies meant to manipulate her feelings?

"How can I believe you?" she asked softly, her heart pounding with a different sort of fear.

"I don't suppose you can." He moved, putting distance between them. Despite the warmth of the afternoon, she felt cooler air pour into the widening gap between their bodies.

Sinclair crept to the edge of the Ghillie net and looked out toward the woods. "Rain's about to start again."

"Lovely."

He eased the edge of the netting up, turning to look at her. "The temperature's cooled down considerably, at least. We'll probably make better time now."

Given the way every muscle in her body screeched in protest at her slightest movement, Ava had her doubts about what sort of time they'd be able to make. But she slipped under the net at Sinclair's gesture and waited for him to fold up the camouflage and store it in his backpack again. She took advantage of the brief pause to look around the woods, trying to regain her bearings. The rain clouds overhead obscured the sun, but there was enough variation in the light to figure out which way the sun was headed.

"Ready?" Sinclair asked, his back to her as he strapped on the pack.

She started to nod when she felt something hard and cool press against the side of her neck. She froze in place, her voice stuck in her throat.

As Sinclair started to turn toward her, a gravelly voice

spoke in her ear. "Do not move an inch. Not an inch." The speaker was male, and his drawl was pure American South, without a hint of a Spanish accent.

Sinclair went still, his eyes slanting toward Ava. They widened slightly as they took in whoever stood behind her. "I really thought you were dead," he said, a quizzical tone to his voice.

There was a hint of shock in the Southern drawl when the man behind her spoke again. "Back at ya, son."

Suddenly, Ava understood the cryptic interchange. "If that's a gun you have pressed to my neck," she said quietly, "please put it down. My name is Ava Trent and I'm an FBI agent looking for you and your wife. You're Gabe Cooper, right?"

There was a brief pause as the man considered her words. After a beat, the gun barrel pressed to her neck fell away. "You're FBI?"

She turned slowly to look at him, biting back a quick gasp of surprise. Gabe Cooper looked, quite simply, as if he'd had the hell beaten out of him. Bruises and abrasions seemed to cover every exposed area of his skin. His nose was swollen and probably broken, bruises already forming under his bloodshot blue eyes. Both lips were split and a little bloody, and bloodstains also marred the torn T-shirt he wore over a grimy pair of jeans. His dark hair was damp with sweat and probably more blood, given the large scrape that extended up his forehead into his hairline.

"Out of the Johnson City R.A.," she answered, looking him over for any hidden injuries. Not that the ones she could see weren't enough to qualify him for a trip to the nearest E.R. "How did you get away?"

"A little luck, a little mulish determination." Gabe's split lips twisted in a wretched-looking attempt at a smile. "I had to kill a man, so I'm a little on edge." He looked past her to Sinclair, who was still standing, stiff-backed, in the same position in which he'd stopped at Gabe's command. "You're Sinclair Solano, aren't you?"

Sinclair's dark eyes slanted toward Gabe. Slowly, he turned to face his brother-in-law. "I am."

Gabe shook his head, grimacing a little at the movement. "She kept telling them you were dead. That they'd taken us for nothing."

Sinclair's eyes closed briefly before he looked away from Gabe and locked gazes with Ava. She felt a ripple of pity for the look of sheer misery on his lean, handsome face.

"This never should have happened," he said bleakly.

"No, it shouldn't have." Gabe looked away from Sinclair, his expression darkening. "Now we have to fix that."

"I'll make a trade," Sinclair said. "Me for her. It's what they want."

"They'll just kill both of you," Ava warned, her gut tightening. "Don't do something drastic and foolish."

"Do you know where they've taken her?" Gabe's voice sounded more slurred than before, drawing Ava's gaze quickly to his face. He'd gone pale beneath his tan, and one hand snapped out to grab the slender trunk of a birch sapling.

Ava and Sinclair moved in tandem to catch him before he sagged to the ground. Gabe tried to push them away, but his movements lacked any strength. While Ava eased Gabe to a sitting position, Sinclair unpacked the Ghillie net and the tent, piecing them together with speed and expert precision. He helped her pull Gabe through the tent flap just as the sky overhead opened up, spilling a hard, cold rain that rattled relentlessly against the top of the tent.

"I'm okay," Gabe protested, but Ava didn't believe it for a moment. A quick check beneath his T-shirt revealed large bruises on his stomach and rib cage. She suspected he had matching marks on his back, as well. He might be bleeding internally for all they knew.

"We need to get him emergency treatment," she murmured to Sinclair.

He closed his fingers around Gabe's wrist, checking the man's pulse. A moment later, he checked Gabe's eyes, frowning. "I don't think he's going to bleed to death in the next little bit."

"Didn't you see the bruises?"

"Yes, but he's not showing signs of blood loss or shock."

"And you're a doctor now?"

Sinclair's gaze snapped up to meet hers. "Believe me, I want nothing more than to deliver him to my sister alive and healthy. But if he's killed one of Cabrera's men like he said, you know there'll be *El Cambio* soldiers out there scouring the woods for him as well as us."

"You know I'm still conscious, don't you?" Gabe asked faintly.

"Go to sleep," Ava said shortly.

Gabe arched an eyebrow in her direction.

"Sorry," she added. "But you really do need to rest. I'm not as convinced as the two of you are that you're not bleeding internally. So do me a favor and take advantage of having someone to watch your back. You need to rest."

Gabe Cooper's eyes darkened as he looked at her, but after a few seconds, he closed his eyes and rolled onto his side with a groan, turning his back to them.

Sinclair nodded for Ava to follow him out of the tent. She crawled out behind him, hunkering down beside him near the edge of the Ghillie net. "When the man who took him out to the woods to kill him doesn't come back, Cabrera is going to send out a search party."

"What makes you think they haven't already? We killed a couple of their scouts, too."

"Yes, but they don't know who we are. They can't know for sure that I'm out here taking out their men. For all they know, we could be local law enforcement, and they'd be careful not to tangle with us if they can avoid it."

"But Gabe Cooper is truly dangerous to them if he makes it back to civilization," she said, understanding his point. "Or if he comes after them directly."

"Everybody in Sanselmo's underworld has heard about the Coopers," Sinclair said quietly. "What they did to Eladio Cordero and his band of drug thugs—"

"Los Tiburones," she murmured. Like anyone involved in law enforcement on the East Coast, she'd heard the story about the Cooper family's skirmishes with one of Sanselmo's most vicious and notorious drug lords. Eladio Cordero had sent his thugs, *Los Tiburones,* after Coopers not once but twice over the course of a couple of years. The Coopers had killed or captured all comers, including Cordero himself, accomplishing what Sanselmo's own national army and police force hadn't been able to do.

"Cabrera knows how dangerous the Coopers are," Sinclair said flatly.

"Then why did he take Gabe and your sister in the first place?" she asked. "Why did he risk it?"

"Because *El Cambio* is on a devastating downswing in Sanselmo," he answered, meeting her curious gaze. "Their popularity has dropped like a stone since the current president's new reforms have started yielding positive changes. All the dire predictions and threats from the rebels have been exposed as desperation from a dying opposition."

"And their tactics have grown more brutal than ever."

Sinclair nodded. "They need a victory."

"How does kidnapping your sister and her husband give them a victory?"

"It doesn't. But using them to smoke me out and take me down?"

"Right." She met his dark gaze, her stomach knotting. "*El Cambio* made you into a scapegoat for half their crimes, didn't they?"

He nodded. "They went through a period after my 'death' where they tried to become a political entity rather than a rebel group."

"It didn't take."

"They weren't patient enough to build a platform. Cabrera wanted power and he wanted it fast."

"So he fell back on violence."

"It's what he knows." Sinclair looked up at the sky through the Ghillie net, releasing a soft sigh. The light drizzle had started to pick up force, becoming a steady shower. Water seeped through the Ghillie net, sprinkling them both with warm rain. "Back in the tent. You don't need to get drenched again."

She followed him back into the now-crowded shelter. Gabe remained on his side, his chest rising and falling in a steady cadence.

"I guess he needed rest more than he realized," she whispered.

"You better get some sleep, too," Sinclair answered quietly. "I have a feeling whatever's waiting for us out there is going to be twice as dangerous as before."

THE DRUMBEAT OF rain on the tent put Ava right to sleep, and Sinclair didn't have the heart to wake her. He knew she'd be angry that he let her drift off again, but she needed the rest as much as Gabe Cooper did.

And he needed to think about what he should do next.

Almost a full day had passed since they'd left Cabrera's camp behind, and while Sinclair wanted to believe the terrorist was going to stay put while he and Ava brought in reinforcements, he couldn't shake the niggling feeling that time was running out for them.

They should have reached civilization by now, if they hadn't been forced to go in circles for a while to be sure they hadn't picked up a tail. Running into Gabe Cooper had only slowed them further, and considering the man's physical condition, he wasn't exactly going to help them pick up any speed.

Meanwhile, Cabrera could be moving Alicia to God only knew where, and Sinclair might never pick up his trail again.

He eased out of the tent, taking care not to wake Ava and Gabe. The heavy rain that had begun falling earlier had eased off to a drizzle again, tempting him from beneath the Ghillie net.

Thanks to the rain, the temperature had dropped several degrees. The air had a clean, earthy smell that reminded him of the mountains of Sanselmo after the afternoon rains. He walked farther from the tent, skirting trees to provide himself some cover, in case someone was out there in the woods watching him.

But he saw no sign of movement. No sounds beyond the steady cadence of rain in the trees overhead. He raised the hood of his camouflage jacket to cover his head and hiked deeper into the woods, away from the tent.

He should have left a note, he realized belatedly. Let Ava know what he was planning. But maybe it was better that he hadn't. She'd just try to follow him. After all, he thought with a quirk of a smile, he was her prisoner.

Alone, taking a chance on a less convoluted path through the woods, he made much better time than he and Ava had made that morning, though he took care to mark his trail with notches in the trees he passed. The last thing he wanted to do was lose the trail back to Ava and Gabe Cooper.

Within an hour, he had reached the bluff overlooking the hidden cove where he and Ava had spotted Cabrera's camp below. He eased to the edge and sneaked a peek over the side. The camp was still there, hunkered silently in the rain. There were two men standing guard outside the tents, their postures tense.

They must have already realized several of their men had gone missing. They would be on high alert now.

He edged away from the bluff and rolled into a sitting position, preparing to rise to his feet now that he was far enough from the edge that no one below could see him.

But as he put his hand down to push to his feet, a flash of movement in the woods to his right froze him in place.

Moving only his eyes, he slowly turned his gaze toward the patch of woods where he'd seen something moving. All was still at the moment, but as he held his gaze steady, a dark figure detached itself from the tree where it had been standing a moment earlier and glided toward the bluff.

One of Cabrera's men, Sinclair decided after studying the camouflage pattern the man wore. It was old-school jungle camouflage, nothing an American hunter would wear here in the Smoky Mountains, especially out of season. And if he were law enforcement, the camo pattern might be even more sophisticated.

The man slipped out of sight, and Sinclair allowed himself a long, slow breath. But before he'd had a chance to do more than exhale, another dark figure moved smoothly into view.

Same camouflage pattern. The man was a few yards closer than the previous one had been, close enough for

Sinclair to get a decent look at his face beneath the streaks of camouflage paint. The shape of the man's nose and the craggy brow gave him away—Antonio Cabrera, cousin to Alberto. As ruthless a bastard as *El Cambio* could offer, and *El Cambio*'s enforcers had been notorious for their brutality.

Sinclair froze in place, closing his eyes to slits as Antonio's gaze slid his way. He held his breath and waited.

After a chest-burning interval, Antonio turned away and headed back into the woods, away from the bluff.

Sinclair allowed himself another deep breath, the only movement he dared. So much for hurrying back to the tent before Ava missed him.

He was well and truly trapped.

Chapter Nine

An early twilight had descended on the woods by the time Ava woke with a start from a dead sleep. She sat up in a rush, her heart pounding in her ears, chased from slumber by a dream she couldn't remember. All that lingered was a sense of imminent danger, as if the fear that had invaded her dreams had retreated only as far as the shadows outside the tent.

"Sinclair," she whispered, trying to calm her breathing, which sounded fast and ragged in the tight confines of the tent.

There was no answer.

She peered around the gloomy interior of the darkened tent. A few feet away, Gabe Cooper was still asleep, his breathing slow and regular. There was no one else inside.

Grimacing as her muscles protested the movement, she crawled to the tent flap and stuck her head outside. The Ghillie net extended another five feet past the door of the tent, but Sinclair wasn't inside the netting.

She rose to a crouch and edged her way to the side of the net, trying to see beyond the camouflage to the rain-darkened woods beyond. She saw no sign of movement other than the steady drumbeat of rain slanting through the canopy of trees.

She had a creeping sense of déjà vu. Here she was,

again, left behind while Sinclair Solano went his own way without telling her what he was planning to do. But this time, there was no plane ticket home, no exciting new career path to take her mind off her woes.

Only dark, perilous woods as far as she could see, full of hidden places where dangerous, well-armed men might be lying in wait.

She slipped back into the tent and edged closer to Gabe, checking the pulse in his wrist. His heartbeat was only slightly faster than it should have been, not fast enough to make her worry that he was losing blood internally.

He stirred at her touch, groaning.

"Sorry, didn't mean to wake you," she whispered.

He rolled onto his back, blinking up at her. "Are we moving?"

"I don't think so."

He pushed himself up on his elbow, grimacing with pain. "Where's Solano?"

"I don't know," she admitted. "I woke up and he wasn't here."

Gabe looked at her a long moment, then muttered a succinct curse.

"Maybe he went out to see if he could find something to eat?" she suggested, wishing she didn't sound quite so pathetically hopeful. She knew damned well that wasn't why he'd left the tent.

He'd decided to go it alone. Just like before. Hell, his mind had already been made up before he'd ever tried to coax her into taking a nap.

Sinclair Solano had a bad habit of doing things his own way, the rest of the world be damned. Clearly, the past eight years had taught him nothing.

"He's not coming back, is he?" Gabe asked quietly.

"I don't think he is," she admitted. His backpack was

gone, although a quick scan of the tent revealed that he'd left two bottles of water with her and Gabe. It might get them back to civilization if they didn't drink too much at a time.

She pushed the thought aside and looked at Gabe. "How're you feeling?"

"Like I ran into a bus."

She rather felt that way herself. "Think you could walk some more before dark?"

He looked around the dim tent. "This isn't dark?"

She checked her watch. "Half past four. We probably have a couple of hours before nightfall."

He stretched carefully, testing his flexibility. From her perspective, he looked as creaky as an old man, but after a moment, he looked up at her and nodded. "I'm game."

Without the backpack, she wasn't sure she would be able to carry the tent and Ghillie net. But Gabe helped her break the tent down and fold it into a compact square. They folded the Ghillie net around the tent and shoved both pieces down the back of Gabe's shirt, holding them in place by tucking in the hem of his T-shirt. He walked hunched over but he reassured her the tent and net were lightweight enough for him to handle.

She put the extra waters in the pockets of her jacket, handed Gabe the MK2 Sinclair had taken off one of the dead Cabrera henchmen, and they started heading west, into a light, damp breeze.

They hadn't gone far, however, before she saw the first sign of a trail through the woods—a nick in the wood of a white birch, clearly a knife mark.

Had Sinclair left a trail for her to follow if they got separated?

She shook her head at first, berating herself for such a hopeless case of wishful thinking. Sinclair didn't want her to follow him. The whole point of leaving while she was asleep was to make sure he got a head start.

Gabe spotted the next notch. “He left a trail,” he said quietly.

She paused by the mark on the fir trunk and looked around. What if it hadn’t been Sinclair who’d left the trail? What if Cabrera’s men were trying to lure them into a trap?

Reaching behind her back, she pulled her Glock from the holster and edged closer to the tree trunk. Gabe Cooper joined her there, the MK2 in hand, his breathing soft but labored.

“You think it might be *El Cambio* instead?” he whispered.

“I don’t know.”

He looked around, his brow furrowed. “I wish I had a way to reach my family.”

“They’re probably already out here somewhere, looking for you.” She looked at the notch on the tree again. “Could one of them have left this mark?”

He shook his head. “That’s not the way we do things.”

“Not the way you do things?”

“We learned not to leave any trace of ourselves. No Cooper would leave a trail like this.”

So maybe it was Sinclair, she thought, mildly disgusted by how much she wanted to believe it was true. Just how stupid was she, anyway? Was she so susceptible to a pair of chocolate-brown eyes and a lean, cut body that she’d forget eight years of fugitive status?

Oh, God, she thought, *don’t answer that. Don’t depress yourself further.*

“Had my family arrived before you came out here?” Gabe asked.

"Not yet. They had farther to come, and I got here pretty soon after your abduction."

Gabe growled at her words. "*Ambush* is more like it. They caught us when I was in the shower. I came out naked and unarmed to find four men with guns pointed at Alicia's head."

Ava felt a shudder of sympathy at the picture he painted. "I'm surprised they didn't just shoot you," she said bluntly. "Clearly that was always the plan—to get you out of the way."

"They didn't want to chance it right there in the motel. And after they got us out into the woods, I think they realized Alicia would cooperate more easily if I was still in the picture. So they took us to their camp before they dragged me off."

"How did you get away?"

"I overpowered the guy with the gun. He pulled a knife, so I shot him." Gabe's answer was flat and unemotional. "What I did will hit me sooner or later, but right now, I don't feel anything but damned glad to be alive."

"You should be," she answered just as bluntly. She'd killed a man herself the day before, and all she felt right now was relieved to be the one still breathing and walking around.

Well, relieved and completely pissed off that Sinclair had gone off on his own, leaving her behind.

He was her prisoner, damn it. What the hell did he think he was doing?

"There's another one," Gabe said, nodding toward a tree about ten yards to the northeast. She made out the notch in the side of the tree trunk.

So far, the trail Sinclair had left them followed a straight northeasterly path. Toward Cabrera's campsite, she realized. They'd taken a twisty, backtracking path away from the bluff the day before, worried about Cabrera scouts following them in the woods, but apparently, Sinclair hadn't been nearly so cautious alone.

"I think he's heading for Cabrera's camp," she said aloud.

Beside her, Gabe's breath hitched. "You know where the camp is?"

She eyed him cautiously. "We know where it was last night. That doesn't mean it's still there."

"The man who took me away to kill me put a blindfold on me." He leaned his head back against the tree trunk, closing his eyes. "I didn't get it loose until we were at least a half mile away from the camp, so I couldn't get my bearings to find my way back to her." He opened his eyes, meeting her sympathetic gaze. "Tell me you saw her last night. Tell me she's okay."

"We saw her. She was alive and very worried about you."

He closed his eyes again. "We've been through so much together. When we met, she was already in danger, and we survived that case. Then she had to go and join my cousin's security agency."

"More danger?"

"We didn't think it would be so much. She works in a consultant capacity. Profiling and forensic psychology. Very behind-the-scenes. I thought it would be okay. I didn't have to be afraid of that kind of job."

"What happened at the motel had nothing to do with her job."

He pushed away from the tree and gazed into the gloomy woods. "No. It had to do with her damned brother."

Despite his injuries, when he moved, there was a gliding grace to his gait, like a wraith floating through the woods. She tried to mimic his stealth as she followed him from marked tree to marked tree, moving closer and closer to the hidden cove where Cabrera had set up camp.

She was the first to see the camouflaged scout about fifty yards ahead. She caught Gabe's arm, wincing in sympathy as he released a soft hiss of pain between his clenched teeth. Nodding toward the man in camouflage, she pulled Gabe back against the wide trunk of a tall Fraser fir.

The man moved in slow, steady circles amid the thick stand of evergreens to their north. He looked more bored than alert, but the AR-15 rifle he carried would make up for any inattention. In comparison, her Glock, with its large-capacity magazine, was outgunned by a long shot. Even the MK2 couldn't compete.

"Look about fifty yards west," Gabe whispered in her ear.

She followed his gaze and saw nothing but trees. It took a moment to realize the clump of bushes near the edge of the bluff was actually a man in a camouflage coat, hunkered down and utterly still. Only the slow blink of his eyes betrayed his presence at all.

And those dark eyes were looking straight at her.

Oh, Sinclair, she thought, her heart contracting with a combination of guilt and empathy. *You came out here to check on your sister.*

His gaze locked with hers for a long moment before his eyes slid half-closed. In that moment, however, a world of communication passed between them. Unspoken words like *Be very, very still. Don't do anything to betray your position.*

"Don't move," Gabe whispered in her ear, his whole body tight with alarm. She froze her position in response, though her eyes slid toward him, trying to figure out what had sparked his sudden tension.

He was no longer looking at Sinclair. Instead, his gaze was locked on to the camouflage-clad scout moving slowly toward their position.

The scout stopped midstep, his head swiveling toward the east. Moving only her eyes, Ava looked where he was looking and saw, with dismay, that Sinclair had moved his position.

He was edging, slowly, stealthily, toward the bluff and the hidden encampment.

Expecting the scout to open fire immediately, she was surprised when he quietly changed directions, heading after Sinclair. If Sinclair realized he was being followed, he showed no sign of it.

"We have to warn him," she whispered to Gabe, already taking a step toward the scout's position.

"No!" Gabe caught her arm, holding her still. "He's leading the guy away from us. He knows what he's doing."

She stared at Gabe, horrified. "He's going to get captured!"

"I think that's his plan."

Stupid man! If Cabrera got his hands on Sinclair, he wouldn't hesitate to kill him where he stood.

"We have to stop this!" she said urgently.

"If we do something now, all three of us will end up dead. We're outgunned and outnumbered."

"So he just sacrifices himself? Do you really think Cabrera will just let your wife go once he's killed Sinclair?"

The bleak look Gabe shot her way answered the question for her.

"We have to stop this," she repeated.

"Are you a good shot with that thing?" He nodded toward the Glock still clutched in her right hand.

"Not from this distance."

"So we have to get closer," he said, already starting to

move, his bruised and bloodied hand tightening around the MK2.

She followed, keeping an eye out for other scouts in the woods. Between her, Gabe and Sinclair, they'd taken out four of Cabrera's contingent of armed soldiers, but there were plenty of henchmen left to worry about. If they weren't careful, they'd all three end up in Cabrera's grasp.

"Solano's heading away from the bluff," Gabe whispered a few minutes later, after their path had wound almost a half mile to the west, away from the encampment. They were about three hundred yards behind Sinclair and the man tracking him, moving more slowly and deliberately to be sure they weren't setting themselves up for an ambush of their own.

"Why hasn't Cabrera's man made a move?" she asked, her tongue thick in her mouth. She hadn't had any water in a while, and she was feeling the effects of thirst.

"I'm not sure," Gabe whispered back. "Maybe they think he's going to lead them to you."

"We're not sure they even know I'm here."

"They know," Gabe assured her. "Just before they dragged me away from camp, Cabrera got a phone call from one of his men, saying he had spotted you in the woods. At least, I assume it was you. Are there any other women roaming these woods packing heat?"

"I shot one of Cabrera's men," she whispered. "Sinclair shot the other, before he could kill me. He also killed a third man."

Gabe turned to look at her, his blue eyes strangely bright in the fading twilight. "They *will* kill us all if they catch us."

"I know."

"So we don't get captured." Gabe turned his head back toward the woods. Ahead, Sinclair's pace had slowed, and the *El Cambio* operative was starting to close the distance between them at an alarming rate.

What was Sin trying to do? Let himself get caught?

Almost as soon as the thought entered her mind, she realized letting himself be captured was exactly what he was counting on. He'd been trying to lure the man away from them the whole time, willing to give himself up to keep them from being found.

Crazy man. For a notorious terrorist, he had an amazingly self-sacrificial code of honor.

"He's going to get caught," Gabe murmured.

"If he does, he's as good as dead."

"Not right away," Gabe disagreed. "Cabrera told his men to bring Solano to him alive."

Her stomach was starting to ache with dread. "He wants to kill Sinclair himself, doesn't he?"

"Yep. Not sure why, but Cabrera really hates Solano."

There was no way they could close the distance between themselves and the *El Cambio* scout before the man reached Sinclair, especially since Sinclair wasn't even trying to stay ahead anymore.

But maybe they could set up an ambush once Cabrera's man had his hands on Sinclair. "We need to split up," she whispered to Gabe.

He looked at the inexorable cat-and-mouse game playing out ahead, then back at her. "Ambush?" he asked quietly.

"We have to try something." She looked away from Gabe, her gaze turning back to the darkening patch of woods ahead where Cabrera's man had closed the distance between himself and Sinclair to less than fifty yards.

Suddenly, seven dark shapes glided out of the trees just behind Cabrera's scout, closing in on him with a mind-shattering combination of speed and stealth. At the last moment, the scout seemed to realize he was surrounded, and the AR-15 came up with a rattle of gunfire.

The sound stopped almost as soon as it started. One sharp bark of gunfire sent the scout sprawling to the ground.

"Well, son of a bitch," Gabe growled under his breath. Ava's gaze whipped up to his face and she saw a slow grin spreading across his face.

"Who are they?" she whispered as he continued smiling.

"Coopers, darling," Gabe drawled, already moving toward the dark figures gliding through the woods ahead. "Who else?"

Chapter Ten

The sight of Alexander Quinn's stony face among his dark-clad rescuers should have been a surprise, but over the past eight years, Sinclair had come to expect the unexpected from his former CIA handler. He'd once joked that he could be stuck at the top of Mount Everest and it wouldn't surprise him to see Quinn in Sherpa gear, climbing to his rescue.

"How'd you find me?" he asked Quinn as the older man left the others to meet him halfway.

"Tagged along with the Coopers." Quinn glanced back at the others who had surrounded the fallen Cabrera soldier. "Want to catch me up?"

As Sinclair started to open his mouth to answer, he caught sight of Ava moving through the woods toward him, her hazel eyes blazing in the fading light. He turned toward her, bracing himself for her fury.

He was not prepared, however, when she launched herself at him, wrapped her arms tightly around his waist and pressed her face to his chest.

He curled his arms around her, his heart pounding as she tightened her grip on his back and rubbed her nose against his collarbone.

"You stupid idiot!" she growled against his shirt, the sound so muffled he wasn't sure he'd understood her.

"Nice to see you, too," he murmured.

She lifted her face away from his shirt, her face glowing with a curious combination of relief and fury. "You were trying to get captured! Have you completely lost your mind? You know Cabrera will kill you on sight."

"He'd kill you and Gabe, too. I wasn't going to let that happen."

"You're lucky that man didn't shoot you the minute he spotted you."

"I didn't figure he would. Cabrera likes to do his own dirty work when it's personal." He smoothed her damp hair away from her pale face. "And what the hell were you doing, following me through the woods like that? If you were in any shape to hike, you should have gone straight back to the motel and called the paramedics for you and Cooper."

"You're my prisoner, remember?" The warmth in her voice was as good as a smile to soften her words. In fact, he thought he heard a hint of exasperated affection in her voice.

"You may need to cuff me," he murmured, deliberately provocative.

Her eyes narrowed slightly before she seemed to realize they weren't exactly alone in the woods anymore. She looked at Quinn, who was watching them with a bemused expression.

"You don't look much like the other Coopers," she said to Quinn.

"That's because he's not one." Sinclair bit back a smile at the way Quinn's eyebrows arched at Ava's acerbic tone. "Ava Trent, this is Alexander Quinn, former spook. Quinn, this is Special Agent Ava Trent with the FBI. I'm her prisoner, it seems."

Quinn's lips quirked slightly before flattening into a neutral expression. "I see."

"Former spook?" Ava asked. "Let me guess. Your CIA handler?"

Even Quinn, with all his years of practice at inscrutability, couldn't hide a flicker of surprise at her words.

Ava's eyes widened as she looked back at Sinclair. "I was kidding."

He shrugged and looked back at Quinn.

"We need to get out of these woods," Quinn said. "Get you all back to civilization and figure out what to do next."

"No," Gabe Cooper said firmly from his position near the other Coopers. "We're not leaving these woods yet. Not until I find my wife."

THE CABRERA SCOUT was dead, taken out by one shot from Rick Cooper's Walther P99. Riley Patterson had been nicked by one of the rounds from the scout's AR-15, but it had caught more jacket than flesh. A large adhesive bandage easily covered the lightly bleeding scratch to his arm, and to her credit, his green-eyed wife, Hannah, seemed to take his injury in stride, as if she was used to seeing her husband under fire.

Hell, Ava thought, maybe gun battles were a daily thing for the Coopers, given the family's reputation for attracting danger.

She was still trying to get all the newcomers sorted out in her head. There were cousins and brothers, including Gabe's twin, Jake, who looked like an unblemished version of Sinclair's battered brother-in-law. He helped his sister Hannah wrap the body of the dead Cabrera henchman in plastic and stash it in the underbrush, while the others spread out, creating a human perimeter around their present position. In the center of that invisible bubble of protection, Quinn quietly debriefed Sinclair and Ava, catching up with all that had happened since Ava walked into an ambush the day before.

She answered his questions, though part of her chafed at being relegated to a grunt in her own investigation. The man was a civilian, for grief's sake. What the hell did he think he was doing, taking over command?

But digging in her heels and trying to assert her command wouldn't really help anything, she realized with frustration. The truth was, she was injured and out of her element. Alexander Quinn and the Coopers had experience dealing with *El Cambio.* Even Sinclair was better prepared to deal with the terrorists than she was.

She was no longer running an FBI investigation. They were running for their lives.

"How many operatives left in camp?" Quinn asked quietly.

"The last time we got a good look, there were nine in the camp. Cabrera and eight others. We've now dispatched five, so eight is probably the most there could be," Sinclair answered.

"It's possible he's sent out other scouts," Ava warned.

Quinn gave her a long, considering look. "Your partner has reported you missing. That probably means we're going to have FBI crawling around these woods sooner or later."

Sinclair groaned deep in his throat.

"Do you have a working phone?" Ava asked.

Quinn's eyes narrowed. "You think calling in is going to put the brakes on the FBI?"

"It might, if I can reach Cade Landry."

Quinn's lips pressed to a tight line, and for a moment, Ava thought he wasn't going to hand over his phone. But finally, he pulled out a slim smartphone and tipped it toward her.

She took the phone and checked the signal. Not great, but at least there were a couple of bars. She dialed Cade Landry's cell number.

He answered on the second ring. "Landry."

"Landry, it's Trent."

Landry muttered a short string of profanity. "Where in God's name are you, Trent?"

"Following a lead," she answered vaguely. "My phone was disabled or I'd have called to let you know."

"There are six agents coming down from Johnson City and Knoxville to look for you."

"Tell them to wait. I've got a peg on where the kidnappers are holed up." That was the truth, at least. "But I don't need an army of suits thrashing their way through here and alerting the perps to our presence."

She thought Landry might argue with her, but to her surprise, he was silent for a moment, then said, "Okay. How much time do you need?"

"A day," she answered after a moment of thought. Surely a day would be enough time for them to figure out how to get Alicia away from Alberto Cabrera. If it took much longer than a day, she had a sinking feeling that Alicia Cooper would no longer be alive.

"I'll try to stall them. Tell them I've heard from you and you're safe." Landry's voice held a surprising hint of concern. "You *are* safe, aren't you?"

"I am," she assured him. "For the time being, anyway."

"Where'd you get a phone?" His earlier concern elided into a flicker of suspicion.

"Long story," she answered.

"You're not alone, are you?"

"No," she admitted. "But I'm not being held captive. I'm with friends."

Landry released another soft curse. "You're with Coopers, aren't you? They're here, you know. Like I warned you."

"I'm with Coopers," she admitted. "And they're good at what they do."

"I won't mention that fact to the suits." Landry sounded resigned.

"Thanks. I'll check back in a few hours to make sure you've been able to keep the suits at bay."

"Your number is blocked. How can I call you back?"

"You can't." She ended the call and handed the phone to Alexander Quinn. "He's going to try to keep the FBI from coming after us."

"Will he succeed?" Quinn asked.

"I don't know," she admitted. "So we'd better figure out what comes next and do it fast."

"What comes next is rest," Sinclair said firmly. "You didn't bring the tent with you, by any chance?"

She looked at Gabe, who was talking to his sister Hannah. "Stashed in the back of Gabe's shirt."

"Smart thinking," Sinclair said with approval as he headed toward Gabe, leaving Quinn and Ava to follow.

"How much has he told you?" Quinn asked quietly.

She glanced at him. "About?"

"His time with *El Cambio*."

"He says he was a double agent."

Quinn didn't respond.

"Was he?"

"What do you think?"

"I think you have a very adversarial relationship with the truth," she answered gruffly, quickening her pace to walk ahead of him.

He simply lengthened his stride and caught up. "He risked his life for this country's interests. For nearly five years. If you believe anything about Sinclair Solano, believe that."

He said nothing more as they reached the others. Sinclair was helping Gabe pull the tent and Ghillie net from his shirt, while Hannah made soft noises of dismay at the sight of her brother's battered body.

"Those sons of bitches," she growled, holding up the hem of his T-shirt for a better look at the darkening bruise over Gabe's left kidney.

"It's all surface," he assured her.

"We need to get you back to the motel and call a doctor," Hannah disagreed.

"He wouldn't still be walking around if he were badly injured," Quinn told her with an air of careless authority that made Hannah bristle.

"I don't need your opinion," she shot back.

"I'm not leaving these woods without Alicia," Gabe said quietly. "Discussion over."

"We have to assume Cabrera will be expecting to hear back from the man we just took out," Quinn said, ignoring them both. "So he'll send more men out here to see what's going on."

"He might try to move Alicia, too," Ava warned. "If he thinks the camp has been compromised."

"All the more reason to go in there and get her," Gabe said sharply.

Hannah put her hand on her brother's arm. "We're outgunned at the moment. We need to be smart about this."

"She's right," Sinclair said.

Gabe looked at him, a scowl on his dark face. "Oh, good. The dead man chimes in."

"You have every reason to think badly of me," Sinclair

said with a calm dignity Ava wasn't sure she could have pulled off in the same situation. "I'm not asking you to like me. But whether you believe me or not, my only concern is bringing Alicia home safely."

"It's your fault she's in this situation," Gabe growled.

"Keep your voices down," Ava warned quietly. "Sound carries."

"She's right." Hannah's fingers curled more tightly around her brother's arm. "We need to do this the right way."

"And you know what the right way is?" Gabe asked.

Before anyone could answer, Hannah's pocket started vibrating. She pulled out her phone, checked the display and answered. "Yeah?"

After listening a moment, she looked from Gabe to Ava, Sinclair and Quinn. "Okay, I'll tell them." She ended the call and put her phone back in her pocket.

"Tell us what?" Quinn asked.

"Jesse wants a powwow."

"I CAN CALL more Coopers in on this," Jesse Cooper said without preamble after he and Luke had joined the others inside the perimeter, leaving Jake, Hannah's husband, Riley, and Jesse's brother Rick to stand watch.

"We're at a disadvantage," Gabe warned. "They're in a sheltered area. It won't be easy to sneak up on them."

"Understood. But we don't have a lot of options." Jesse worked while he talked, helping Luke and Hannah set up three lightweight tents. Taking a cue from them, Sinclair set up his own tent as well. "We may need to consider negotiating with them."

"Cabrera's not a guy who likes to settle for anything less than what he wants," Sinclair warned.

"And what he wants is to get his hands on you." Gabe gave Sinclair a long, considering look.

"No," Ava said flatly. "That's not going to happen."

"You don't get to make that decision." Sinclair put his hands on her shoulders, turning her to face him.

There was very little moonlight seeping through the occasional breaks in the cloud cover overhead, making it difficult for him to see her expression. But the stubborn jut of her jaw made it clear: she had no intention of supporting his plan to offer himself in a trade for his sister.

She grabbed his arm, her grip strong. "You know it's not that simple. There's no guarantee he'll let her go if he gets his hands on you."

"We can make a straight-out trade part of the deal," he insisted. "They don't get me until she's safe."

"He won't go for that."

"He might. He wants his revenge, and clearly, he's taken a hell of a lot of risks to make it happen. Kidnapping a married couple from a motel and hauling them into the mountains isn't exactly the act of a rational man."

"The dead man had a radio," Jesse interrupted, moving closer to where Sinclair and Ava stood. "Maybe we can contact him that way."

The scudding clouds overhead parted briefly, revealing enough moonlight that Sinclair caught the glare Ava shot Jesse's way. For a woman who'd spent most of the past two days swearing her only interest was bringing him to justice, she seemed pretty invested in keeping him alive.

If only the situation were different....

But it wasn't. Nothing that happened in the next day or so would change the mistakes he'd made. They would never pay for the lives he'd harmed, directly and indirectly. He wasn't going to get a happy ending, and it was time he accepted that fact.

"Why don't we do this?" Jesse said after a long moment of tense silence. "Let's get some shut-eye. Sleep on it. We'll take turns patrolling the perimeter and send out regular scouts to the bluff to make sure Cabrera doesn't bug out on us."

"I'll volunteer," Sinclair said. "I can show you where the camp is."

"We've already located the camp," Luke said quietly. "We went looking for it earlier, while we were sweeping the woods. We have the GPS location set in all our phones now."

Sinclair grimaced. If he'd bothered to keep his phone charged, he might have been able to record the camp location rather than hoping he'd remember how to find it. So much for being his sister's hero. He apparently had trouble finding his backside with his own hands.

"Rest is a good idea." Ava's voice interrupted Sinclair's moment of self-pity. She closed her hand around his biceps and gave a little tug, making him look at her. Her hazel eyes glittered in the filtered moonlight that made her skin look as cool and smooth as porcelain.

"You're going to stay in the tent with me?" he asked.

"You're my prisoner, remember?" A hint of a smile softened her words. "Am I going to have to whip out my handcuffs to make the point?"

"Ooh, would you?" He shot her an exaggerated leer, pleased when she smiled in response.

"Come on." She lifted the flap on the tent and led him inside.

He sat across from her, cross-legged, his knees touching hers. "How's your hip?"

She made a face. "Feels like someone set it on fire and poured alcohol on it, thank you very much."

He didn't like the sound of that. He'd done his best to

clean the wound when it happened, but considering how much they'd been traipsing through the woods over the past couple of days, infection remained a valid threat. "Maybe I should change the bandage. It might be getting infected."

"Not much we can do about it if it is."

"We can get you back to Poe Creek before it gets out of hand."

She shook her head. "You're not benching me on this case."

"Would you rather die of infection?"

"It's not that bad, really." She winced as she shifted position.

"Let me look." Sinclair caught her chin between his fingers, making her meet his gaze. "Some fresh disinfectant and a new bandage may be all it needs, but I have to take a look to know for sure."

She closed her eyes briefly, as if warring with herself, before she unzipped her trousers. Wriggling them down over her hips, she turned on her side, exposing the now grimy bandage he'd taped to her hip the day before.

He removed the bandage as gently as he could, bracing himself for what he'd find beneath it.

"Well?" she asked.

"Not as bad as I feared." The wound, while not appreciably better, was no worse. "A little inflammation, but no obvious infection to worry about. I think we cleaned it up in time. Think you're up for another cleaning?"

She groaned low in her throat. "Oh, why the hell not?"

He grabbed his backpack and pulled out his first aid kit, frowning as he realized he was dangerously low on some supplies. Of course, the hyper-prepared Coopers out there probably had a mini-hospital packed in their supplies if he needed something.

He gathered what he needed and set to work cleaning the edges of the bullet furrow, wincing in sympathy with each of Ava's soft gasps. "Sorry. I know it hurts."

"I'm fine," she gritted. "Just get it done."

He felt almost as relieved as she looked when he patted down the last piece of tape and sat back on his heels. "There you go. How's it feel?"

She shot him a dark look. "How do you think?"

"Terrible?"

She pushed to a sitting position, trying to tug the waistband of her pants back up. But they had become twisted while he was treating her injury, and each tug made her hiss with pain. "It'll be okay by morning."

"Or worse," he warned. "Day two after an injury is almost always worse than day one."

"Thank you, Mary Sunshine," she muttered.

"Here, let me." He tugged her up to a kneeling position. From there, he helped her straighten her trousers so that they slid easily up over her hips.

Her breath burned hot against his cheek, and when he met her gaze, her hazel eyes seemed as dark and deep as midnight. "Thank you," she whispered.

His whole body seemed to contract to one pulsating pinpoint of sensation, his blood coursing like lava in his veins. He felt viscerally conscious of the smallness of the tent they shared, of a turning point not unlike that moment in Mariposa eight years ago, when he'd been forced to make a quick decision about which way his luck would turn.

And despite the myriad reasons why he should leave her again, this time he feared he didn't have the strength to walk away.

Chapter Eleven

Ava pressed her palm against his sternum. His pulse hammered against her hand, rapid and strong. She felt a vibrant hunger radiating from him, consuming her, swallowing her whole. Somehow, she found enough breath to whisper, "Do you remember that morning when you showed me the canal near the base of Mount Stanley?"

"Yes." His breath stirred her hair, a potent reminder of the way he'd held her that morning on the mist-shrouded canal as they watched the sky turn brilliant colors—mango, salmon, vermillion—as the sun burst over the horizon into the azure sky.

She leaned closer, her cheek brushing his. "Sunrise, remember?"

"I remember." He turned his head until his lips touched her temple. "You told me I was a heathen for knocking on your motel room door so early."

"I was on vacation." She smiled at the memory of her grumpy reaction and his youthful enthusiasm. She'd been angry at him, at first, for dragging her out of bed so early.

And then she'd seen the dark fins break the mirror surface of the canal. One, then two, then a half-dozen, arcing their way through the water in a graceful, soul-stirring dance.

"You were right," she admitted, rubbing her cheek

against his beard bristle again, reveling in the raspy sensation. "It was worth getting up early to see the dolphins run."

He ran his fingers lightly across the skin exposed by her open-necked blouse. "I didn't tell you the whole truth."

Despite the ripple of apprehension his words evoked, she couldn't suppress a shudder of sheer, sensual response to his artful touch. "The whole truth about what?"

"The dolphins didn't run only at sunrise." He brushed his lips against the curve of her cheekbone. His lips were firm, yet soft. She couldn't stop herself from leaning in to his caress. "They ran all the time, morning, during the day, even late at night. I just wanted to see the sunrise with you."

She tipped her head back to look at him. "I've always been such a level-headed person. But you shot that to hell and back, you know? Even after I knew what you'd done, who you'd become, there was a part of me who just couldn't stop wanting to spend another Mariposa sunrise with you."

Sometimes, she'd dreamed of that morning, over and over, as if she could somehow find the right combination of words and touches to keep him with her always.

But she always awakened alone.

He cradled her face between her palms, making her look at him. "Tell me you want me to kiss you. Just like I kissed you that morning. Tell me."

Fear shimmered in her chest, but it was just one of the sensations rocketing through her, and not the strongest. Desire was stronger. Longing was stronger.

Too strong to still the words hammering at the back of her throat. "Kiss me, Sin."

Curling his hand around the back of her neck, he tugged her closer and dipped his head, brushing his lips lightly against hers.

A soft, low sound escaped her throat. Pressing closer, she clutched the sides of his T-shirt in her fists and kissed him back. No hesitation. No reserve. Just a hot, sweet, wet kiss that made her head reel and her heart race.

He dropped one hand to the hem of her shirt and slipped his fingers between her blouse and the flesh beneath, tracing the ridges of her rib cage until he reached her back. "You're so soft," he whispered as he dragged his lips away from hers to press light, teasing kisses down the curve of her jaw. "But you're also strong." He splayed his hand against her spine, his fingers pressing against the muscles of her back. "Fit."

Her seldom-worn skinny jeans might beg to differ, she thought, but she wasn't going to argue with a man whose tone suggested he found her damned near perfect.

"Solano?"

For a moment, she thought she'd said his name herself. But the voice sounded again, a little louder. Just outside the tent. "Solano?"

Sinclair drew away from Ava, his breath coming in staccato rasps. He gazed down at her, his eyes impossibly dark and his expression diamond-hard with desire. "Damn it," he whispered.

"Solano, are you awake?" It was Hannah Patterson. At least, Ava assumed so, since she was the only other woman in their camp.

Ava nodded toward the tent flap. "Better answer your door."

With a groan, he crawled to the tent opening and pushed it open. Hannah stood outside with Alexander Quinn.

"What is it?" Sinclair asked, his eyes narrowed.

"We just got a call from our people at the motel. Someone broke into Agent Trent's motel room and ransacked the place."

Ava groaned. She'd left her things with Cade Landry, including her notebook computer. Had he put those things in her room?

"What that means," Quinn added, his expression grim, "is that Cabrera now almost certainly knows he's dealing with an FBI agent."

Beside her, Sinclair released a soft profanity.

"What am I missing?" Ava asked.

"A lot, apparently," Quinn answered.

"If there's anything Cabrera hates as much as he hates me," Sinclair explained, "it's the FBI."

"Why's that?" Ava asked.

It was Alexander Quinn who answered. "That, Agent Trent, is a long and sordid story."

WHILE HANNAH JOINED her husband and her brother Jake on the perimeter, Jesse and Rick Cooper gathered with their cousin Luke and the others in the center of the small camp, passing around sticks of beef jerky along with a large thermos of hot coffee and several disposable cups. Sinclair poured a half cup for himself and the same for Ava, while she tore into one of the beef jerky sticks.

She looked worried, he thought, and bone-tired. But she was alert enough to ask the obvious question that should have occurred to him. "Is Agent Landry okay?"

Quinn looked surprised by the question. "They didn't bother him. He spotted people in camo leaving your room, but they got away before he could retrieve his gun and go after them."

"And they didn't shoot at him or anything like that?"

"Maybe they didn't want to draw any attention to themselves."

"Did they take anything from the room?"

"Landry wasn't sure what had been in your bags. He

said the computer was still there, but it was out of its bag, plugged in and turned on."

Which answered one question, Sinclair thought. They'd been looking for something specifically about her. "I wonder how they knew she was an FBI agent to begin with?"

"I guess they knew we were in town and did a little snooping around. I didn't even think to check those first two bodies for radios—did you?" she asked Sinclair.

He nodded. "The three we killed definitely didn't have radios on them. But that doesn't mean the others don't."

"How much critical information was on your laptop?" Jesse asked.

"At a glance, not a lot. But it would have information about my relationship with the FBI. They might not easily get into the system, but they could easily enough figure out that I'm FBI connected."

"Maybe that's what they wanted to know," Quinn suggested. "They know someone's out here. I think they're pretty sure Sinclair is one of those people, but they must know he has an accomplice."

"You make it sound like we're the criminals," she grumbled.

Sinclair couldn't stop a smile. "According to you, at least one of us is."

"We can worry about who's guilty of what after we get Alicia out of there." Gabe Cooper's raspy voice came from behind Sinclair's shoulder. He turned to find his brother-in-law standing near the tent where he'd been sleeping, a blanket wrapped around his shoulders. He looked battered and wobbly on his feet, but he shrugged off his brother Luke's offer of help and limped to join their conversational circle.

"Here." Luke unfolded a camp chair and made his

brother sit. "We're trying to figure out the best way to get to Alicia without putting her in more danger."

"He wants to kill me," Sinclair said bluntly, tired of pretending there was any other possible approach to their problem. "He took her to lure me in. So we should use it."

"How? By handing you over like ransom?" Ava shook her head. "That's not an option."

"Why not? She wouldn't be in that camp with Cabrera if it weren't for me. So let's give him what he wants."

"Negotiating with a terrorist never works," Ava argued.

"Sometimes it does."

She was furious with him; he saw the anger blazing in her eyes, turning them as dark as night.

"Agent Trent is right," Quinn said, breaking the tense silence. "Cabrera will just kill you both if you hand yourself over."

"So let's set up an exchange in neutral territory. Open-field exchange, no weapons allowed," Sinclair suggested.

"You're expecting a man like Cabrera to honor that arrangement?" Ava looked at him as if he'd lost his mind.

"He's not going to honor anything like that," Quinn agreed.

"There has to be a way we can make this happen." Tension built in Sinclair's chest until he felt as if his heart was going to implode from the pressure. Alicia had already been with Cabrera for over twenty-four hours. God only knew what he had already done to her. For all they knew, she wasn't even alive anymore, and he was just standing here as if anything mattered besides getting her to safety.

"What if we set up a meeting between you and Cabrera?" Quinn suggested.

Ava wheeled to face the former spy, her shoulders squared. "No way. If Cabrera gets within shooting distance, he'll kill Sinclair and ask questions later. For God's sake, you *know* that!"

"We *don't* know that," Sinclair disagreed. "If there's one predictable thing about Cabrera, it's that he's unpredictable."

"All the more reason we don't risk putting you in the line of fire," she countered, whirling to glare at him. "This isn't a movie. The bad guys don't stand there and give a long speech about their motives before they start shooting. And good guys don't miraculously survive their wounds."

Sinclair leaned closer, touching his fingertips lightly to the curve of her waist just above her injured hip. "Sometimes they do."

"Stop," she growled, although her features softened as he dragged his fingertips around her to settle lightly against her back. "Please."

"I think he might have questions." Sinclair tried to keep his tone reasonable as he dropped his hand back to his side, even though he was chafing against Ava's dogged caution. "He has to wonder if I was the only double agent in his organization. He may think I can finger others."

"Double agent?" Jesse Cooper asked.

Sinclair looked at him, realizing everyone else here, besides Quinn, still thought he was a traitor. Pressing his lips in a thin line, he glanced at the former spymaster, who watched him through narrowed eyes.

"He was working for the CIA for the last five years of his time with *El Cambio,*" Quinn said after a long pause. "It's not widely known, and if you ask the CIA, they'll deny it. But it's true. I handled him during his time undercover."

Sinclair looked at Ava, trying to gauge her reaction. She looked back at him, her expression thoughtful.

"Well, hell." Gabe Cooper was the first to speak, his voice coming out in a raspy grumble. "Does Alicia know?"

"Of course not," Sinclair answered. "I couldn't let anyone know the truth. It could have jeopardized everything."

Gabe shook his head. "She blamed herself for your death, you know."

"What? Why?"

"She says the last time she talked to you, she told you she hoped you blew yourself up in your next bomb."

"Oh." Sinclair rubbed his jaw to hide the flare of old pain that raced through his chest at the memory. "I didn't blame her for that. I blamed myself. As far as she knew, I deserved her disgust."

"She doesn't see it that way." Gabe limped closer, all broad shoulders and belligerent anger. "You have a lot to account for where she's concerned. And don't think your CIA bona fides are going to wipe it all away."

"I don't," Sinclair assured him.

"But they *do* matter," Ava said quietly. "And if it's possible that Cabrera suspects you were a CIA double agent all that time, it's even more insane for you to put yourself out there as a target for him."

"Well, whatever we decide to do, we aren't going to do it before morning." Jesse stepped forward, a commanding presence that even Sinclair, who grew up challenging authority at every turn, couldn't ignore. The elder Cooper had a calm demeanor, an inherent sense of competence, that probably made him one hell of a CEO for a global security company.

He almost gave Alexander Quinn a run for his money.

"Let's sleep on it," the former spy agreed. "We'll take turns manning the perimeter. Four-hour shifts."

"Hannah, Riley, Jake and Rick can cover the next three

hours," Jesse said. "Luke, Quinn and I will spell them at one."

"And at five?" Ava asked.

"You're injured. No guard duty for you. And Sinclair is a target, so no duty for him." Jesse sent Sinclair a look that quelled his argument before he could make it. "At five, we'll regroup and figure out what we plan to do." Jesse gave a brief nod that everyone else seemed to read as a dismissal. They retreated to their tents.

Unfortunately, Sinclair thought as he followed Ava back to the tent, the perimeter guards meant he couldn't easily sneak out of camp to negotiate his own deal with Cabrera.

"You're not thinking of sneaking out, are you?" Ava asked quietly a few moments later as they settled into the cramped confines of the tent.

He couldn't hold back a smile. "What, you read minds now?"

"I read people," she answered, her tone serious. "Part of my job training, you know."

"It's more than your training," he contradicted her, tugging off his hiking boots and wiping them down with a towel from his pack. He picked up her discarded boots, wiping them as well. "One of the first things I noticed about you that first day in Mariposa was how easily you seemed to see past all my outer bluster to the person underneath. It was...disconcerting. And maybe a little exhilarating."

"I didn't read you all that well, in the end." Her quiet tone might have seemed neutral to most people, but maybe he had a little of her people-reading ability as well, for he could sense a layer of pain beneath the words.

"You read me too well," he disagreed, touching her cheek. Making her look at him. "I almost called to tell you I'd go with you on the hike we'd planned that day. I had time before the meeting my father set up with Grijalva. But I knew, deep down, that if I gave you the chance, you'd see what I was up to, that you'd talk me out of meeting Grijalva at all. So I didn't give you the chance."

"I wish you had," she murmured.

He touched her cheek, wishing he'd made a lot of different choices. "So do I."

She closed her hand over his, holding it in place. "So you really were a double agent for the CIA."

"Nah," he said with a smile. "That would be a cliché."

A reluctant smile curved her lips, carving dimples in her cheeks. He'd almost forgotten about those dimples, the way they took ten years off her face and made her look like a mischievous girl instead of a fully grown woman.

Those dimples had disarmed him the first time he'd seen them, years ago on a Mariposa beach. They hadn't lost their power.

He leaned closer, pressing his lips against one of those tiny indentations. "You should get some sleep. Tomorrow's going to be a long day, I think."

She moved her thumb across his chin, her skin making a soft rasping sound against his two-day growth of beard. "I don't think I trust you not to hare off on your own."

He couldn't blame her for that, he supposed, since he'd been thinking of doing that very thing only a few minutes earlier. "I don't suppose I'd be able to sneak past the Coopers anyway," he said with a shrug.

With a soft sigh, her shoulders slumped and she dropped her hand away from his face. "But you'd like to."

It would be easy to back away right now, he thought. Put distance between them, ease the ache of longing that seemed to come with spending time with her. She made him want things he knew, deep down, he couldn't have.

Didn't deserve to have, and certainly not with a woman like her.

But this might be all the time he'd ever get with her. Even if things went perfectly, if he and the Coopers managed to come up with a foolproof plan for getting Alicia back without trading his own life for hers, there was still no chance of a future with Ava Trent. She was an FBI agent and, regardless of the true situation, he was and would always be considered a traitor and a fugitive. Hell, if he just remained a dead terrorist, it would be the best possible outcome.

He put his fingers under her chin, tilting her face up. Willing her downcast eyes up to meet his. After a silent battle of wills, her eyelashes fluttered up to reveal her warm hazel eyes, full of vulnerability and questions.

"I don't intend to go anywhere tonight." He brushed his lips against hers, keeping the touch tender but undemanding. "So let's get some sleep."

She lowered her gaze, turned so that she was lying on her uninjured side and stretched out across the padded bedroll that covered most of the tent floor. Her body rose and fell in a gusty sigh.

He lay next to her, close enough that the heat of her body washed over his own. He edged nearer, until his hips cradled her round backside. Feathering his fingertips down her arm, he whispered, "Is this okay?"

Tension coiled in her body for a long moment before she relaxed, curling herself against him. "This is good," she murmured.

He snuggled closer, wondering with a sinking heart how he was ever going to walk away from her a second time.

Chapter Twelve

The world was dark when Ava woke with a start, chased from slumber by a hazy, ill-remembered nightmare that left her heart pounding and her breath burning like fire in her lungs. For a moment, she couldn't remember where she was or why she was there. A low throb in her hip suggested an injury, and the answering ache in her head suggested a bone-tired weariness.

Then she remembered everything, in a swirling rush, and her pulse ratcheted up another notch as she realized Sinclair was no longer there with her. Which meant—

The tent flap opened, and Sinclair's face appeared in the gap. "The Coopers have coffee going. Want some?"

"God, yes," she muttered, trying to hide her relief at seeing him.

She must not have succeeded, for as he helped her ease her aching body through the narrow tent door, he whispered, "You seem surprised to see me."

She managed a smirk, not willing to let him see just how glad she was to find him still here instead of off in the woods somewhere playing martyr. "Not really. I just figured I'd wake up to find you hog-tied somewhere after the Coopers caught you trying to breach their perimeter."

"Hannah's got a sort of latrine set up behind her tent. Thought you might prefer that to a bush in the woods." He arched his eyebrows at her as he pointed her toward Hannah's tent, making her smile a genuine smile.

When she returned to the campsite, Sinclair had a cup of coffee and a cereal bar waiting for her. There were also more people in the camp, she saw with surprise—more Coopers, by the looks of them. They eyed her with curiosity while Jesse Cooper made the introductions.

"Ava, this is my sister Isabel and her husband, Ben, my cousin J.D. and his wife, Natalie. Izzy and Ben are Cooper Security agents. J.D. flies our company bird, and Natalie is a deputy sheriff." He nodded at Ava. "This is Special Agent Ava Trent with the FBI."

"Don't pretend you'll remember us all." Natalie stepped forward with a quirky grin to shake Ava's hand. She was a tall, muscular woman with friendly green eyes and a mane of wavy auburn hair pulled back in a utilitarian ponytail. "I still get them all mixed up after two years."

"Maybe y'all should wear name tags," Ava answered with a smile as she sat in one of the camp chairs Sinclair had procured for her. They huddled in a semicircle around a small kerosene camp stove that was heating a fresh pot of coffee.

"We'll take that into consideration." Jesse's smile belied the sharp watchfulness in his blue eyes. As she'd noticed the night before, he seemed to carry his role as CEO with him wherever he went, taking charge with the ease of a man used to command. Probably former military, she surmised, taking in his straight spine and broad shoulders. Marine, maybe. Or Special Forces. A man who exuded competence and authority.

Gabe Cooper was looking marginally better that morning after several hours of sleep. Having his siblings around seemed to infuse him with extra energy as well, adding a little spring to his limping gait as he settled in the folding chair next to his twin, Jake. He looked across the small circle at Sinclair for a long moment before speaking.

"I want my wife away from that crazy bastard Cabrera. And it may not be fair of me to say so, Solano, but I'm willing to let you take a risk with your life to get her back."

Ava put her hand on Sinclair's arm and shook her head. "It's not a smart plan."

"With all due respect," Jesse said in a quiet but firm tone, "you haven't actually heard our plan yet."

Biting back a retort, she pinned her gaze on the Cooper Security CEO. "So spill it."

He met her gaze without flinching, his expression hovering between annoyance and amusement. "We set up the exchange with Cabrera. A neutral meeting spot. Armed escort for Solano."

She shook her head. "Not good enough."

"I'm not finished."

Sinclair put his hand on her knee, giving it a light squeeze. "Let him talk. I'd like to know what he's got in mind myself."

"You don't know?" She shot him a look of surprise. She'd assumed Sinclair and the Coopers had discussed everything while she was sleeping and were presenting it to her as a fait accompli.

Jesse walked over to stand in front of Ava and Sinclair. "Solano, you can say no. We'd rather you didn't, but we're not going to shanghai you into playing bait against your will."

"Speak for yourself," Gabe muttered.

Jesse slanted a warning look at his cousin. "We think Cabrera will bring an armed contingent with him, as well. In fact, we'll offer that as a part of the deal—we'll have five armed people escorting Solano. He can bring the same number for himself."

"He has seven men left, if we're right about how many he brought with him," Ava murmured.

"He's fond of even numbers," Quinn said, echoing what Sinclair had told her before. "I'd guess he brought an even dozen. That comports with what Gabe saw before he was dragged out of the camp."

"We figure he'll leave two in camp to guard Alicia," Jesse added.

"Ah," Solano murmured.

"We go in the back door, overpower the two remaining guards and get Alicia out of there," Jesse finished.

Ava nodded, realizing it *was* a pretty good plan. At least, it would be if Cabrera fell for it. And if they were right about how many remaining men Cabrera had with him.

More ifs than she liked.

"Cabrera may not go for it," Sinclair warned, echoing Ava's concerns.

"I think he'll risk it to get his hands on you." It was Luke Cooper who spoke that time, in a low voice that rang with certainty. "I know how people like Cabrera think. Believe me, I've had experience with blood vendettas."

He was *that* Cooper, Ava thought. The one targeted by Eladio Cordero. He'd tangled twice with Cordero and *Los Tiburones* and lived to tell.

"He'll take any chance to get his hands on you," Luke continued. "He won't be able to help himself."

Sinclair shook his head, his dark eyes troubled. "What keeps him and his men from killing the lot of you as soon as they set eyes on you?"

"It's a chance we're willing to take to get Alicia out of there alive," Jesse answered for his cousin. "And we've got better weapons now, too." He nodded toward his cousin J.D., who started handing out rifles and ammunition magazines. AR-15s, mostly, fitted with high-capacity magazines, similar to those some of Cabrera's men carried. "This should make us at least even. Gabe says they don't seem to be wearing protective vests, so they're not going to be invulnerable to our bullets."

"You're talking about a paramilitary assault in the middle of Tennessee," Ava protested.

"Yes. We are." Jesse met her gaze without flinching. "Can you deal with it?"

As much as she didn't want to admit it, she knew what he and the others were planning was quite possibly the only workable solution to their problem. The FBI couldn't take the same risks to save Alicia that the Coopers would. And the Coopers were a hell of a lot more motivated than the government to get Alicia out alive.

"Okay," she said after a long pause. "But I want in on it."

"You're injured," Sinclair protested, closing his hand more tightly around her knee.

"I'm fine," she disagreed, ignoring the twinge in her hip. "And I have no intention of twiddling my thumbs in the tent while everyone else gets in on the action."

"Actually," Jesse said, "if you're good with a rifle, we could use another person on the extraction team."

"No," Sinclair said.

"Cabrera won't take women seriously," Luke explained. "So we're putting all men on the front team. J.D., Jesse, Rick, Jake and Ben will go with you. Riley took a bullet hit last night, so he and Hannah stay here with Gabe."

"Oh, hell, no," Gabe growled. "You're not benching me."

"Gabe, you're not in any condition to be an asset. You stay here," J.D. said firmly. "Riley and Hannah stay with you. You three guard the camp and call for reinforcements if things go belly-up."

"Natalie, Quinn, Luke and I were going to be the extraction team at Cabrera's camp," Jesse's sister Isabel said. She was tall and slim, with deep brown hair pulled back in a ponytail like Natalie's and eyes the color of strong tea. It took a moment for Ava to realize she'd met Isabel before, several years ago.

"You were an FBI agent," she blurted as Isabel's gaze met hers. "We met at a conference six years ago."

Isabel nodded. "I wondered if you'd remember."

Her heart contracted as she remembered something else about the former FBI agent. "Oh, God. Your partner was killed in that explosion in Maryland, wasn't he?"

"Um, actually—" Isabel's husband, Ben, cleared his throat.

"My partner." Isabel waved her hand toward Ben with a quirk of a smile on her face. "Not so dead after all." She slanted a look at Sinclair. "Seems to be a lot of that going around."

Apparently, Ava thought. "So, if I join the extraction team, that's five against hopefully two."

"The more the better," Jesse said. "In case we're wrong about how many men Cabrera has with him."

"Ava is injured," Sinclair said sharply. "She took a bullet to the hip."

"It was a scratch," she protested as the Coopers all turned to look at her. "It's already healing."

Luke gave her a considering look. "Will it stop you from being useful in the raid on the camp? Tell me the truth."

"It's painful, but it's not debilitating. I can do the job."

Sinclair caught her arm and pulled her aside. "It's not just your wound you need to think about," he said quietly.

"If you participate in this raid, you could get in serious trouble with the FBI."

"I know," she answered. "But I can't sit here while y'all risk your lives to get Alicia back. I didn't join the FBI to be hamstrung by rules." She'd been thinking about that aspect of her job for a while now, especially on the days when it seemed she spent more time filling out forms than solving crimes. "I'll deal with the fallout when it comes. But for now, I need to be useful. There are lives at stake. And if we can take out Cabrera here and now, that could save a whole lot of lives back in Sanselmo, as well."

He brushed his knuckles against her cheek, his touch light but the expression on his face dark with emotion. "I don't want anything to happen to you."

"I don't want anything to happen to me, either," she said with a lopsided smile that made his lips curve in response. "Trust me that I know what I'm doing. I've been on raids before." She didn't elaborate that most of them had been carefully controlled scenarios during training. The training was still valid, and she knew what to do. "I can do this."

"If we're going to do this, we need to start getting everything set up now," Jesse Cooper warned from a few feet away.

Ava turned to face him. "Then let's do it."

BY 9:00 A.M., Jesse Cooper was ready to make the radio call to Cabrera's camp. The others gathered close around him while he thumbed the speaker switch and spoke Spanish into the radio microphone.

After a long pause, the radio crackled, and a voice on the other end asked in guttural Spanish who was contacting them.

"I want to speak to Cabrera," Jesse answered. "Only Cabrera."

There was another pause before a second voice came over the radio. "I am Cabrera," the voice declared. Jesse looked at Sinclair.

Sinclair nodded, his chest tightening at the sound of his old foe's voice.

"This is Jesse Cooper. We have Sinclair Solano. We're willing to trade him for Alicia Cooper, but we must have evidence that she is still alive and well. Put her on the radio."

"You don't make the rules." Cabrera's tone was pure arrogance, fitting the man Sinclair remembered. "How do I know this is not a trick?"

"We have one of your radios, so you know we've dispatched one of your men," Jesse said coolly. "But if you want to speak to Solano, that can be arranged." He looked up at Sinclair, raising one dark eyebrow.

Sinclair nodded and took the radio. "Cabrera. You want me, you can have me, but only if you let Alicia go."

"Your sister is a beautiful woman," Cabrera said in a tone designed to make Sinclair's skin crawl. Across from him, Gabe Cooper lurched out of his camp chair, held back by his brothers Jake and Luke. Jesse shot his cousin a warning look.

"You're a lot of things," Sinclair said in a voice far calmer than the rage boiling inside his chest, "but you're not a deviant. I have your word as a soldier that you haven't touched her in an inappropriate way?"

"As you say," Cabrera said, "I am not a deviant. She is our guest."

"Then let her go. I will come to you willingly if you let her go."

"I cannot afford to believe you, Sinclair. You have not been the most honorable of men in the past, have you?"

He supposed, from Cabrera's point of view, that fact was inarguable. "I have betrayed you and *El Cambio*. But I'm willing to face your justice now if you will let my sister go unharmed."

"In due time," Cabrera said. "I assume you have an offer more reasonable than the one you just gave me?"

Jesse took the radio from Sinclair. "We'll bring Sinclair to a neutral place in the woods. There's a partial clearing we found last night." He rattled off some coordinates; Sinclair guessed one of the perimeter teams had scouted out a place for the exchange the night before and marked down the GPS coordinates. "I have five men with me besides Solano. You may bring five men of your own. We'll meet and make the exchange."

"We will meet," Cabrera agreed after a pause that lasted so long Sinclair feared the terrorist leader had decided to end the conversation abruptly. Releasing his breath, he sought and found Ava's dark-eyed gaze. Her lips curved in a scared smile, and he closed his hands into fists to keep from grabbing her and pulling her into his arms right here in front of the Coopers.

"Eleven-hundred hours?" Jesse asked.

"As you wish," Cabrera answered. "It would not be a good idea to double-cross me."

Jesse exchanged a look with Sinclair, his expression grim. "You'll have Alicia with you?"

"Of course."

Sinclair shook his head. Cabrera was lying. The question was, did Cabrera know they were lying, as well?

"He may have a trap set if he believes we plan to trick him," he warned Jesse after the other man had shut off the radio.

"Entirely possible," Jesse agreed. "It's a risk we have to take. Everyone in the extraction team has been trained for high-risk situations." He looked at Ava. "At least, I assume the FBI took the time to give you some training?"

"Of course," she answered. "In fact, my first SAC came from the FBI's Hostage Rescue Team, and he was convinced all FBI agents should go through similarly rigorous training. He got our unit into an HRT training course as part of a Homeland Security initiative," Ava said. "It was hard, but I learned a lot about thinking and acting under pressure." She looked first at Jesse, then at Sinclair. "I can do this. I'm prepared."

At the moment, all Sinclair wanted to do was wrap her in cotton and stash her somewhere far from here where she couldn't get hurt. But she wouldn't be Ava Trent if she weren't willing to take risks to help people in trouble. Hell, the first time they'd met on the beach in Mariposa, she'd been helping a little girl find the parents she'd wandered away from. Sinclair had helped her track down the frantic parents and reunite them with their adventurous offspring.

He had to let her do what she was trained to do. Trust her to know her limits.

Trust her to come back to him.

And then what, Solano? What if you get Alicia back and Ava comes back safely? You're still a wanted fugitive. Remember?

No happy endings.

Chapter Thirteen

An hour later, Ava slipped back into the tent she and Sinclair shared to find him sitting cross-legged in the center of the small space, his head down and his shoulders slumped. Looking up, he scooted over to make room for her. "How was the planning meeting?"

"We think we have most of the bases covered," she answered, reaching across the narrow space between them to take his hand. "How about you? Scared about playing bait?"

"My idea, remember?" He gave her hand a little squeeze. "All that matters is getting Alicia back to her husband safe and sound. And getting you back to the FBI in one piece."

"That's not all that matters." Her fingers twined through his, her grip strong. "I want you safe, too."

A hardness in his eyes made her stomach ache. "Ava, you know this won't end well for me, no matter what happens."

"Do you have some sort of martyr complex? Is that why you joined *El Cambio* in the first place? Because I don't understand why you value your life so little. You did an amazingly brave thing, working for the CIA the way you did. You probably saved countless lives by keeping *El Cambio* in check all those years." She tugged his hand, her chest tight with frustration as she saw how little her words seemed to affect his sullen mood. "Sin, look at me."

His dark eyes slowly rose to meet her gaze. "There's so much you don't know."

"Then tell me."

He looked away, shaking his head. "There are things I can't tell you because they're classified. And other things I don't want to tell you because they're sources of shame."

"Is that why you haven't tried to clear your name? You think you deserve only bad things from here on out because you made a mistake when you were in your twenties? That's crazy! This whole country was built on the notion of second chances. People can be very forgiving if you give them the chance, Sin. Give them the chance."

"You don't know what I did."

"I'm pretty sure I know most of what you did," she said quietly. "I made it my business to know."

His eyes met hers, dark with dismay. "Made it your business?"

"Not many FBI agents have a vacation fling with a terrorist-in-the-making. It was an anomaly I couldn't resist investigating."

He looked down. "You must have been so disgusted with me."

"I was," she admitted. "And a little disappointed in myself, too. I've always prided myself on my good judgment about people, and there I went, falling hard for a radical with violent tendencies."

"If it makes you feel better, it was the violence that opened my eyes."

"You didn't know they were violent when you joined? You had to know at least some of what they'd been doing in Sanselmo."

"Grijalva sold it as civil disobedience. Vigorous protest taken too far now and then by misguided, desperate *campesinos*."

"And despite everything in the news about *El Cambio*'s acts of terror, you bought that?"

"My parents raised me to question everything, including what I hear on the news. The media is eminently manipulable. Meanwhile, Grijalva was a man of ideas and principles."

"Who was co-opted by men with homicidal intentions."

"Yes. He looked the other way a little too willingly. And he paid for his mistakes with his life."

She could tell from the tone of his voice that Grijalva's death had affected him deeply. "You saw Cabrera kill him, you said."

"I couldn't reach them in time." His voice sounded as bleak as a prairie in winter. "I suppose I'm lucky—Cabrera would have shot me on sight if he'd seen me."

"What did you do?"

"I just wanted to get the hell out of there. Go home and face my mistakes, whatever the cost. So I walked three miles to the capital and turned myself in to the U.S. Consulate in Tesoro."

"Where you met Alexander Quinn."

He nodded.

"That explains your conversion," she said after a moment of tense silence. "But a lot happened in the eight months before you saw the light. You were involved in property destruction, according to the FBI records. *Before* you became a double agent." She didn't know why she was pressing him to admit his crimes; they both knew what he'd done, and none of it was really pertinent to their current problems.

But it mattered, she realized, if there was going to be any chance of a relationship between them that lasted past rescuing his sister. Maybe she was crazy to even think of such a thing, but the truth was, she'd never forgotten Sinclair Solano. He'd been part of her life for years, even after his alleged death. She still had her research notes on his life with *El Cambio.* If she'd ever told her superiors about all the background work she'd done on the group, she might even have talked her way onto one of the FBI's antiterrorism task forces.

But she'd kept Sinclair Solano a secret. Hid his memory in her heart, where it had ached like a splinter for years.

"What do you want from me, Ava?" Sinclair pinned her with a dark glare, as if he could see right through her. "Do you want me to tell you that what I did wasn't really so bad? I can't do that. I designed pamphlets full of pretty lies that led people away from hope into destructive envy. I aided and abetted destruction of property that ruined livelihoods, if not lives. I blew up nine men—and as far as I'm concerned, it doesn't really matter that they were terrorists. I killed them." He passed his hand over his face, as if he could rub away the horror that twisted his expression. "And I made a deal with the devil in order to bring my former friends to their knees."

"I'm not sure Quinn would appreciate being called the devil."

"Quinn knows what he was. What he is."

"Is he why you're here in Tennessee?" she asked. "You didn't come here for your sister—you were already here. No way you could've gotten to that crime scene so fast if you weren't already in the area, especially since you appear to be getting around on foot these days."

"Quinn asked me to do some things for him."

"For his private investigation agency?"

"No, it was something he had going on the side before he quit the CIA." Sinclair shrugged, as if he didn't know quite how to describe what he'd been doing for Quinn. "I was keeping an eye on some bad people. Just reporting to Quinn if I saw something out of the norm."

"Are you still doing that? Is that why you're here?"

"The bad guys are dead now. Anyway, I ran into someone who recognized me a few months back. So I went to ground."

"But you stayed here in Tennessee."

"I like the mountains," he said simply. "They remind me of Sanselmo."

The longing in his voice plucked at the sore place in her own heart. "You miss Sanselmo. In spite of everything."

"In spite of everything," he agreed. "It's a beautiful country. With beautiful, generous people. I regret the pain I caused those people with my stupidity, and I know I can never go back there again. But sometimes, I still dream of the mountains of Sanselmo and I wake up feeling as if I've lost a piece of me."

"I'm sorry."

"Don't be sorry for me," he said sharply. "I made my own bed."

She sucked in a deep breath and took the plunge. "What will you do after this?"

His gaze rose to hers slowly, his expression wary. "After this?"

"When we get Alicia back to her husband. What will you do then?"

"I don't know. Head somewhere else, I guess."

"Why not stick around?"

He shook his head. "I can't clear my name, Ava. The CIA isn't going to vouch for me, and while I might be able to dodge any federal charges, with some help from Quinn and others, my name is ruined. I have nothing to offer anyone."

"Quinn could hire you at his agency."

"To do what? Even if I managed to sort out the mess of my life, my face and name would be imprinted in the minds of the public. What kind of detective do you think I'd make?"

"There are other jobs besides undercover work. You could be an analyst, or—"

He caught her arm, gave it a light shake. "Stop it, Ava. You can't fix me. Don't beat your head against a wall trying."

"So I'm just supposed to watch you walk out of my life again without trying to stop you?" She clamped her mouth shut, realizing too late that she'd revealed more about her thoughts and desires than she'd intended.

"Yes." He lowered his head, his shoulders heaving with a long sigh. "That's exactly what you need to do."

"I don't accept that."

His gaze snapped up, blazing with frustration. He caught her by her arms and gave her a gentle but frustrated shake. "Why can't you let this go? Don't you understand how toxic I am to anything I touch?"

"Don't be so damned melodramatic." She jerked away from his grasp, trying to gain control over her own burst of anger. "Do you think you're the first young radical who's done a few things he regretted? Please. Just look at your parents."

He opened his mouth to protest, but she saw the moment the realization hit him.

"They were part of the Journeymen for Change," she elaborated. "A group who set bombs across U.S. cities in protest against the government and for change. And yes, those bombs even killed a couple of people. Maybe your parents didn't set those bombs themselves, but they supported the causes of the people who did and tried to protect them from prosecution."

His eyes narrowed. "You know a lot about my parents."

"I told you. I made you a subject of study."

"And my sister? What do you know about her?" There was a note of hunger behind his question, she realized, as if he was eager to hear what she had to say.

"She was harder to pin down," Ava admitted. "She didn't live as public a life as your parents. I know she was an excellent student. I knew she'd gotten her masters recently, but I didn't know she'd married into the famous Cooper clan." One reason why she hadn't immediately made the connection with Sinclair.

"My parents must hate that she married an Alabama bass fisherman with close ties to law enforcement and the military." A reluctant smile nudged the corners of his lips upward.

"What do you think about it?" she asked curiously.

"I think Gabe Cooper obviously loves her like crazy, and his family is willing to put a lot on the line to protect her. I might wish her life was a little less adventurous, but that was never Ali's style." His expression when he spoke of his sister was warm enough to heat the tiny tent. "If my parents can't appreciate that, it's their loss."

"I think you should give people a chance to see who you are now, not the misguided man you were eight years ago." She risked touching him again, letting her hand slide slowly upward to rest lightly against his hardened jaw. "And maybe you need to give yourself the same chance. Take a good look at who you've become. Who you are *now* matters, you know. Nobody's life should be judged on one foolish mistake."

"Foolish mistake," he murmured, not moving away

from her touch. His lips curved in a humorless smile. "I think that's painting it a bit kindly."

"I'm not sure it is," she disagreed, letting her hand fall away. There were a lot more things she'd like to say to him, but he already had a lot to think about, and very little time left before he had to go out there and put himself in the crosshairs of a vindictive killer's sights.

She'd just have to hope they'd both live long enough for her to tell him everything else she wanted to say.

In the meantime, she needed to get ready for her own coming challenge. If she and the others in the extraction team didn't do their job, the risks Sinclair was about to take would mean nothing at all.

"THANK YOU."

Sinclair looked up to find Gabe Cooper standing in front of him, looking even more battered than he had the day before, now that his bruises and scrapes had had time to reach full color. His left eye was swollen to a slit, and he apparently had some swelling in his mouth, because the words came out a little thick-tongued. But the clarity in his blue eyes was unmistakable.

"Don't thank me," Sinclair said darkly. "Alicia wouldn't be in this mess if it weren't for me."

"I learned a long time ago that doing the right thing comes with risks," Gabe said. "From what Quinn tells me, you did the right thing in a very bad situation. There are consequences. But I'll tell you this—as much as I hate the fact that Alicia's out there in trouble because of what you did, I know she's going to be damned glad to know you're alive. And that's even before she's had a chance to learn that she was wrong about you all this time."

"She wasn't wrong. Not exactly."

"I think she'd disagree." Gabe extended his hand. "I

haven't been a fan of yours. I guess time will tell if we'll ever really feel like family. But the fact is, you didn't have to put your neck on the chopping block for her this way. If you were the man you seem to think you are, you never would've offered. So, thank you. And good luck."

Sinclair shook his brother-in-law's outstretched hand, feeling a strange sense of his life starting to spiral out of his control. He'd spent the past six months hiding from the world like wounded prey because a man named Adam Brand now knew he was alive. One extra person in on the secret had been enough to send his high-strung fight-or-flight instincts into a tailspin.

Now a whole extended family would know the truth. His sister would know. There was no way he could ask her to keep the secret from his parents, once she knew—it would be unfair to ask her to do so.

Like it or not, Sinclair Solano was alive and kicking once more, and there wasn't a damned thing he could do to change it.

"You worried?"

He closed his eyes at the sound of Ava's soft query coming from behind him. Turning slowly, he opened his eyes and met her concerned gaze. "A little, I guess. Mostly for Alicia."

"I'm going to be the one to get her out of the camp," she told him. "The others are in charge of taking out the camp guards."

He brushed his fingertips against her cheek. "She'll be in good hands."

"I know you don't think there's any sort of future for you—"

"Ava—"

"Just hear me out." She licked her lips and took a deep breath, looking like a nervous student who'd memorized a big speech and was going to get it said, come hell or high water. "I know you think you're in a dead-end situation. I understand why you feel that way. I do. But you have options. There are people who can and will help you if you'll let them."

"Have you ever considered," he asked, "that maybe I don't deserve anything but a dead-end situation?"

She stepped closer, her voice lowering to a whisper. "Do you think I idealized your memory after you left? Do you think I watched the reports of *El Cambio*'s crimes come rolling across the news feeds and thought, 'Oh, Sinclair's different! He must have good intentions. If only I could tell the world the truth!' Not even close. I hated you. I wanted you caught and punished. I was disgusted with myself for being sucked in by you in Mariposa. So believe me, I've more than considered it. I spent years cheering for your capture and punishment."

Her words rang with truth. And with a bleak undercurrent of old resentment that made his stomach twist into a painful knot.

"But I have more information now," she added in a gentler tone, meeting his gaze without flinching. "And I spent a few minutes talking to Alexander Quinn after we finished our final walk-through of the extraction plan. I know the courage it took for you to stay undercover with *El Cambio*." She lifted her hand as he started to speak. "Just don't. Don't try to tell me I have it all wrong. Do you think the CIA was ignorant of what you did even before you turned yourself in? You were a propagandist. And a bloody fool. But you weren't a terrorist."

"I helped terrorists, Ava. It's close enough."

"You were duped by them into providing aid. That is *not* the same thing."

"People died either way," he growled.

"So to honor their memory, you're going to throw yourself on your sword? How does that honor them?" She caught his hand, wouldn't let go even when he tried to tug his fingers out of hers. "Just think about what I'm saying, okay? We're going to get your sister back. And we're going to all get out of here alive. So you're going to have a future to think about, you hear me? And you'd better start deciding now how you plan to live it."

He meant to let go of her hand, but when he moved, it was to grasp her fingers more tightly in his. "You be careful, okay? Don't make me regret agreeing to this plan."

She rose to her tiptoes and pressed her mouth softly against his. As kisses went, it was quick and almost chaste. But the fire blazing in her hazel eyes when she drew back and looked up at him set off dozens of earthquakes along his nervous system.

"Think about what I said," she murmured, squeezing his hand briefly before she released him and walked over to where the others in the extraction team were waiting for her.

He watched her go, his heart swelling with an unexpected flourish of something he hadn't felt in a long, long time.

Hope.

Chapter Fourteen

The eastern side of the hidden cove where Cabrera had made camp was a gently sloping hill rather than a bluff. Accessible by backtracking through the woods and climbing over a rocky incline for a good half mile, the eastern approach was riskier than the bluff that sheltered the cove to the west. But once Ava and the rest of the extraction team saw their chance to make a move, getting into the camp would be a lot easier than trying to scale the side of the bluff without taking fire from the guards.

Communication consisted of cell phones set on vibrate. Less bulky than radios, J.D. Cooper explained, and quieter, as well. Hannah lent her phone to Ava for the extraction. She was to wait until the others engaged with the guards before she went to the central tent, where Cabrera seemed to be keeping Alicia.

First, however, they had to receive confirmation from Jesse that Cabrera was on the move with his entourage.

They spread out along the slope, about twenty yards from the outer perimeter of the camp, and hunkered down to wait for the signal. All five of them were dressed in camouflage well suited to the terrain and the time of year; even though Ava knew where the others were supposed to be, they were nearly impossible to make out against the scrubby mountainside.

Her hip was giving her hell, but she forced herself to remain utterly still. Surprise depended on stealth. She wasn't going to be the one to blow this extraction, especially not with Alicia's life on the line. Sinclair and his sister deserved a chance to make peace and, maybe, forge a new bond.

She damned well intended to give them that chance.

The phone in her hand vibrated. Slowly, she looked down at the dimmed display. There was a text message from Jesse Cooper.

Go.

It was the signal. It meant Jesse had eyes on Cabrera and his men, and that Alicia was not with them, as they'd anticipated. Nobody had expected the ruthless terrorist leader to actually keep his word. It's why they'd planned for an extraction in the first place.

Like wraiths gliding through the woods, J.D., Natalie, Isabel and Ben moved in a semicircle around the camp. Jesse had armed them with high-capacity rifles as well as pistols, since the guards would probably be similarly armed. Ava's role was to get to Alicia and get her out of the camp, so she made do with the MK2 Sinclair had taken off one of the men who'd ambushed them their first day in the woods.

She heard a shout arise from the other side of the tents. The extraction team had been spotted.

The others no longer bothered with stealth, drawing the guards their way, away from the tents. It was Ava's signal to move.

She ran toward the central tent, staying low to avoid detection and to stay as clear as she could from any crossfire if the guards began to exchange fire with the rest of the team. Though they were pretty sure Alicia was being kept in the middle tent, she checked the other tents as she went, just to be sure.

When she finally came to the center tent, she paused outside for a second, catching her breath. Adrenaline poured through her, setting her nerves ablaze, but a hint of dread crept into the mix, freezing her in place a few seconds longer than she'd intended.

What if Alicia wasn't inside the tent? Or worse, what if Cabrera had killed her already?

Gritting her teeth, she pulled open the flap of the tent.

Someone flew at her, slamming into her injured hip and knocking her to the ground. Pain flared through her like a lightning bolt, and for a second, she couldn't breathe.

Hands and feet pummeled her, then pulled away. As Ava turned toward her attacker, the bundle of fists and boots coalesced into a slim, dark-haired woman sprinting through the open tent flap and disappearing outside.

Ava pushed herself to her feet and took chase.

"He doesn't have Alicia with him," Jesse warned as he returned to where Sinclair stood near the shelter of a tall maple tree that was already beginning to change color, its leaves taking on the first hints of future autumn splendor. "We knew that would probably be the case."

Sinclair nodded, but the knot in his gut tightened another notch. Now he had to face an almost certain firefight while his mind and heart were firmly in Cabrera's camp, where his sister and Ava were in mortal danger.

"Your sister isn't alone, you know." Luke Cooper stood

a few feet away, his gaze directed toward the woods. Cabrera and his men hadn't come close enough for a visual yet, but Sinclair could feel them out there. Ruthless. Relentless. Driven by rage at what *El Cambio* saw as a betrayal of the worst kind.

"I know." His voice came out low and strangled.

Luke spared him a quick glance. "What made you change your mind about *El Cambio,* anyway?"

"Seeing them in action," he answered bluntly. "Realizing just what I had signed on for."

"Rebellions always look better on paper," Luke murmured before he once again fell silent and watchful.

"Tangos five o'clock," Jesse murmured.

Even as his gaze swept northwest in search of whatever Jesse had seen, it took a moment for Sinclair to remember that *tango* was military slang for *terrorist.* Half the Coopers had done time in the military, if memory served.

He spotted the first of Cabrera's crew moving slowly through the woods toward them. It was impossible to recognize anyone from such a distance, so he didn't worry himself with who Cabrera might have on his advance team. Cabrera was the one to worry about.

Three other camouflage-clad men came into view before Sinclair spotted the compact, muscular man bringing up the rear. Sinclair's gaze locked on the last man, certain to his bones that he was watching Alberto Cabrera. The man had a cocksure walk, a powerful, charismatic presence that drew the eye to him automatically.

"Cabrera," Luke Cooper murmured.

"There are only four men with him," Jesse said in a hard tone. "There were five earlier."

Sinclair's gaze slid away from Cabrera, counting the other men in sight. Jesse was right. Four men.

"Either he sent someone around to flank us," Luke murmured, "or he sent someone back to the camp."

Jesse pulled out his phone and typed something quickly while dividing his attention between the approaching men and the phone. He slipped the phone back into his pocket. "Sent an alert to the extraction team." He motioned for Rick and Jake to peel off behind them, in case Cabrera was circling someone around to surprise them from the rear.

Sinclair wasn't worried about their rear flank—he had seen enough of the Coopers in action to feel safe that they could handle anything Cabrera threw their way.

It was the unknown, volatile situation back in Cabrera's camp that had his heart climbing into his throat.

ALICIA COOPER WAS faster than Ava would have thought, fleeing through the thick underbrush with remarkable speed and agility. Ava's injured hip shrieked in protest as she kicked her speed up a notch and set out after the woman she was supposed to be saving.

Suddenly, a flurry of movement in the bushes not far from Alicia sent Ava's heart rate spiking. A man in camouflage swung through the tangle of mountain laurel bushes blocking his way, his rifle barrel rising.

She had little time to aim, but Ava brought up the MK2 and fired a shot toward the man with the rifle. The man dived into the underbrush, swinging his rifle toward Ava.

Ava spared a last look at Alicia, who was zigzagging through the woods away from her and the gunman, before she started shooting and running away from camp in a desperate gamble that she could lure the gunman after her rather than Alicia.

The gamble worked. As soon as she put a little distance between her and the man in camouflage, he came crashing through the underbrush after her, Alicia forgotten, at least temporarily.

She kept moving, flitting between trees to keep cover between her and the man with the rifle, but a few shots zinged entirely too close to her for comfort. Worse, the trees were starting to thin out a bit as the ground began to rise upward, healthy evergreens displaced by dead and dying trees suffering from blight.

As she scanned the woods ahead for her best options, she heard a loud buzz right by her ear. Pulling back, she saw the culprit—a honeybee flitting around her head. A moment later, she saw two more, wheeling and circling near a large hive hanging from a low branch of a nearby hardwood tree.

Hunching her head down, she hurried past the beehive and ducked behind the broad trunk of a moribund Fraser fir several yards up the trail. Breathing hard, she dared a glance back toward her pursuer.

He was thirty yards back but moving quickly. She was losing ground, and her brief slowdown when she encountered the bees hadn't helped.

She aimed her MK2 at the *El Cambio* rebel coming up the hill toward her. "Halt and surrender," she called out in Spanish.

Her answer was a quick trio of shots from the man's rifle, kicking up splinters from the tree offering her cover.

She was never going to be able to outgun him, she realized with a sinking heart. And even if he emptied the rifle, he almost certainly had plenty of extra ammunition on him. She, on the other hand, had only what remained in the magazine and chamber of the MK2. She needed backup, but she'd left the others behind in the camp, dealing with the two guards who'd been watching Alicia.

Her gaze darted back to the beehive again, an idea forming. Lifting the MK2, she waited, her heart in her throat, for the man to slip behind the tree where the hive hung. As she'd expected, he kept close to the trees, using them for cover just as she had. But she didn't need to hit the terrorist.

She just needed to hit the beehive.

The distance wasn't optimal, but the hive was large and its bee-covered profile easy to pick out in the woods. The second the terrorist darted behind the tree holding the hive, she fired the MK2. It bucked in her hand, and for a moment she thought she'd missed.

Then the beehive fell from the tree and hit the ground, splitting open and spilling a cloud of angry honeybees into the air.

She heard the man behind her reel off a rapid-fire stream of profanity in Spanish. Peering out from behind the Fraser fir, she saw the man in camouflage running away, beating his arms around his head and shoulders. Squinting, she could just make out dozens of dark spots flitting around his head, hovering and diving.

Within minutes, he was out of sight, retreating back toward the camp, beating bees off him as he ran. Ava stayed where she was a few minutes longer, just in case he thought about doubling back, then started picking her way through the woods, steering clear of the area near the broken beehive as she tried to regain her bearings.

She'd been running east most of the way, so west would take her back to the cove. South would take her in the direction Alicia Cooper had been running. As she started heading that way, a vibration against her hip sent a jolt through her nervous system before she remembered Hannah's phone tucked in her pocket.

She pulled it out and saw a text message from J.D. Cooper.

Location and status?

She punched in an answer and hit Send. A second later, a message popped up, informing of a message send failure.

"Damned mountains." Shoving the phone in her pocket, she kept moving south.

CABRERA STOPPED FIFTY yards away, barking a command to halt to his four companions. "Be a man, Solano!" he called. "Face me alone."

Sinclair looked at Jesse. "Any news from the camp?" he asked softly.

Jesse shook his head. "Not yet."

"When my sister is safe, I'll meet you anytime, anywhere," he called back. "Those are my terms."

The faint crackle of a radio signal carried across the space between them. One of the men pulled out a radio and spoke rapidly into the receiver. A moment later, the man crossed to Cabrera's side and spoke softly into his ear. Sinclair wondered if they were getting word of the attack on the camp.

Was Alicia safe? Had the extraction worked?

Why hadn't anyone called in yet?

"You're a liar," Cabrera called out. "You will pay for your deception."

Before they could move, Cabrera and his four soldiers turned and started running away, toward the camp.

"Son of a bitch!" Sinclair started after them.

Luke Cooper grabbed his arm, stopping him after a few steps. "We just got the signal. Everybody's clear of the camp. J.D. and the others have Alicia. She's safe."

Sinclair's knees trembled beneath him. He held on to Luke's arm to keep from falling. "Are you sure?"

"Just got the confirmation signal from Isabel," Jesse said, crossing to where Luke and Sinclair stood. Jake joined the cluster as well, though Rick, Sinclair noted, remained vigilant, watching the woods where Cabrera and his men had disappeared.

"What about Ava?" Sinclair asked.

"She hasn't signaled in yet, but they definitely said they had Alicia, and it was Ava's job to get her out of there, so—" Jake paused at the sight of Sinclair's scowl. "I'll see if I can reach her on the phone."

"Thanks."

"We need to bring in the FBI now. Let them round up Cabrera and his men," Luke said. "We came for Alicia. No point in putting ourselves at further risk when the Feds can handle it from here."

"Agreed." Jesse frowned at the phone.

"What's wrong?" Sinclair asked, watching Jesse with growing dread.

"She's not answering any texts," he answered. He pushed a few more buttons. Seconds later, his phone vibrated. "J.D. says she didn't check in when they sent a request for a status update."

"Damn it!" Sinclair scraped his fingers through his hair, adrenaline building inside him until he felt as if he were about to explode. "This thing isn't over until we find Ava."

"Cell coverage is spotty in the mountains," Luke said, his reasonable tone doing nothing to quell Sinclair's anxiety.

"I'm going to find her." Sinclair started hiking south, toward the area where the extraction team had made their approach.

"Cabrera will kill you if he finds you," Jesse warned.

Sinclair stopped and looked back at the Cooper Security CEO. "Not if I find him first."

"I'll come with you," Luke said, starting after him.

Sinclair turned and put his hand up. "Rendezvous with the others as planned. Get Alicia out of here safely. I'll find Ava and we'll meet up with you as soon as possible."

Luke held out his cell phone. "At least take this."

Sinclair took the phone. "Thanks."

"Call if you need us." Luke looked as if he wanted to say more, but Sinclair didn't give him the chance. Picking up speed, he headed deeper into the woods, his pulse pounding in his head.

He should never have let Ava be part of this plan. He should have taken her straight back to the motel that first day, his own safety be damned.

He just hoped she wasn't about to pay for his mistakes.

SHE WAS LOST. Utterly, hopelessly lost.

Ava faltered to a stop by a fallen maple tree and sat on the crusty trunk, wiping perspiration out of her eyes and wishing she'd brought a bottle of water with her. But she and the rest of the extraction team had agreed to travel light in order to move with the most speed and stealth.

Great idea, until someone gets lost.

The sun had been approaching its zenith when dark clouds blew in from the west and covered it. Impossible to know for sure, without the position of the sun to guide her, if she was even still heading south.

She rather doubted it, since she'd been hiking for what felt like nearly an hour without coming across the rendezvous site they'd agreed on. Worse, she was getting no cell coverage now, not even a single bar, and the GPS program utterly refused to cooperate in giving her some sense of her bearings.

Maybe she should just stay put. Wasn't that what the experts said to do when you got lost in the woods? Stay put and let people find you.

The Coopers would wonder why she hadn't phoned in. They'd come looking for her. All she had to do was wait.

Except there were more people in these woods than Coopers. What if they hadn't been able to round up Cabrera and his men? What if he was still here somewhere in the woods, looking for his now-missing prisoner and the people who had stolen her from him?

He might consider an FBI agent a pretty good substitute. A hostage, at least, to get him out of these woods and on his way to the safety of Sanselmo's deep, green jungle.

If she kept sitting here, waiting for someone to rescue her, she might end up on the wrong end of an AR-15 with no way to protect herself but a handgun she could barely shoot straight.

She peered up at the overcast sky, trying to discern a lighter spot, an area that might reveal the position of the sun.

After a couple of moments, the clouds thinned out, revealing a faint hint of blue sky and the unmistakable glare of sunlight somewhere to her left. She checked her watch. Ten after noon. At this time of year, the sun would already be dipping toward the west.

Which meant that south was dead ahead.

All she had to do was keep going straight, and sooner or later, she'd find her way back to the Coopers.

WITHIN THIRTY MINUTES, Sinclair was descending the sloping southern approach to the cove where Cabrera had hidden his camp. He moved slowly, kept close to trees and bushes providing cover, well aware he wasn't as camouflaged as the extraction team had been.

The camp was still. According to the plan, J.D., Isabel and the others were supposed to subdue the camp guards and leave them tied up in the camp for the mop-up. Sinclair supposed it was possible that Cabrera had already found his men incapacitated and freed them, but if he had, there was no sign of them there in the cove.

The tents were still there, however, and for a moment, Sinclair wondered if Ava could be tied up inside one of them, a new captive Cabrera could hold over Sinclair's head.

It wasn't possible that Cabrera knew how much Ava had come to mean to him. But if nothing else, Cabrera probably had a pretty good idea just how strong Sinclair's sense of responsibility could be. After all, he'd put his life on the line for five years to make up for a year's worth of youthful stupidity and destruction, hadn't he?

Cabrera might be willing to gamble that Sinclair would trade himself for almost anyone he could take captive.

The central tent had been the one where Cabrera had been keeping Alicia. If he had Ava, that's where he'd be keeping her, as well.

There was only one way to find out, he realized, his pulse quickening with a combination of fear and determination.

He had to go into the camp and look.

Chapter Fifteen

She was definitely not going south anymore, Ava decided as she took one more faltering step and realized, with alarm, that she was fewer than thirty yards from the sheltered cove where Cabrera had set up camp. The tops of the tents were visible from where she stood frozen in place.

And there was someone moving around down there.

Easing behind the closest tree trunk, she bent down, trying to figure out at what point she could no longer see the camp. If she moved in a crouch, she decided, she could get to the next tree down the slope without being spotted from the cove.

Before she moved, she checked her phone. Bars! She punched in a quick answer to J.D. Cooper's earlier status request, then rose just far enough to see what was going on below in the camp.

She'd been right. Someone was definitely moving around down there, gliding from tent to tent. She caught a glimpse of dark hair, a patch of camouflage, the sharp angle of a cheekbone.

Her heart skipped a beat.

It was Sinclair. What on earth was he doing in Cabrera's camp?

She started forward, then went utterly still, her gaze snagged by movement across the camp. A broad-shouldered man of medium height swept his way toward the encampment, showing no sign of stealth or concern, only a singular, relentless intent evident in his dark face. Though she'd seen only a blurry photo once several years earlier, she knew gut-deep that she was watching Alberto Cabrera heading straight for the raided camp.

And Sinclair Solano.

If she called out to warn him, she might alert Cabrera to his presence as well as hers. But if she remained silent, Cabrera might catch Solano by surprise.

The cell phone she'd almost forgotten vibrated in her left hand, giving her a start. Swallowing a gasp, she tucked herself more firmly behind the tree trunk offering her cover and looked at the display.

The text was from Jesse Cooper.

Your GPS display shows you're at Cabrera's camp. Get to cover and do not move. Cabrera and his men are as yet unaccounted for.

Tell me about it, she thought, her gaze moving back to the camp. Cabrera had reached the floor of the shallow cove and was moving without hurry to the area where the tents were clustered.

A crackling noise to her left drew her gaze away from Cabrera. A second man stepped into view in the woods west of her, his gaze on the encampment a few dozen yards down the gentle slope. He had a rifle in one hand, ready if needed, and he spoke something low and unintelligible into the radio in his other hand.

Ava heard the crackle of a radio drift up to her position and realized it must have been Cabrera's handset. She could no longer see the terrorist leader, but if she'd heard the sound, then Sinclair surely had. He'd know he was no longer alone in the camp.

But how on earth could he get out of there without being caught?

The henchman had now moved close enough that Ava could hear Cabrera's reply through the radio he held. Enough of her rusty Spanish lingered in her memory to decipher what he was saying. "The camp guards are missing as well as Solano's sister. I've sent the others out to find them. Join Esperanza in the south. Go."

Though in most cases it was hard to make out nuances through the distortion of the radio, there was no way to miss the anger in Cabrera's terse reply. The man in the woods wheeled around and started back from where he came.

One down, Ava thought, eyeing the camp again. One left. Between them, she and Sinclair might be able to overpower Cabrera.

But only if Cabrera didn't shoot first and ask questions later.

"WHAT AREN'T YOU telling me?"

The rising tone of Alicia Cooper's voice drew Quinn's attention away from the woods for a moment. Gabe Cooper's pretty young wife, though pale-faced and grimy from her ordeal, seemed otherwise uninjured. But she could tell Jesse and the others weren't telling her everything they knew.

"Just tell her," he said bluntly, returning his gaze to the tree line in search of intruders.

"Is Gabe badly hurt? Is that what you're keeping from me?" Her voice rose with alarm, to Quinn's dismay. Despite evading Cabrera and his men thus far, they weren't entirely out of danger, not as long as the terrorist and his crew of bandits still roamed the woods.

The Feds were taking their own sweet time getting there for the mop-up. Not that Quinn was surprised; one reason he'd left a job he'd otherwise loved for so many years was how increasingly hidebound the federal bureaucracy had become, making it nearly impossible to carry out the only mission that really counted—protecting American freedom.

But really—how long could it take to get a crew of FBI agents from Knoxville or Johnson City? An hour? They should already be here. But they'd have to set up a staging area and swing their badges around until they got their pecking order straight, and by then, Cabrera and his gang of not-so-merry men could have taken half the county hostage.

"Gabe has bruises and abrasions. Maybe a cracked rib. But he's already starting to heal up," Jake assured her in a quiet tone. "You know how tough he is."

"I wish he didn't have to prove it quite so often." Her voice lowered back to a soft murmur, almost too low for Quinn to catch. A moment later, however, he heard her voice again from just a couple of feet away. "What do you want them to tell me?" she asked.

He glanced down at her, struck by how much she looked like her brother, despite the differences in them. Solano was tall and slim, like his elegant mother, while Alicia had inherited her father's short stature and heavier build. On her, the extra pounds looked good, located in all the right places and kept in check by her boundless energy and self-discipline. But she and Solano shared the same soulful dark eyes, the same olive skin and raven-wing hair. And in those brown eyes, he saw the same sharp intellect that had convinced him to give her brother a second chance all those years ago.

"Quinn," Jesse Cooper warned.

Quinn ignored him. She was tough and she had a right to know the truth. "They're not telling you that your brother, Sinclair, is alive and he's here in Tennessee."

Behind her, Jake Cooper's expression darkened with anger, and somewhere nearby, one of the other men muttered a curse. But Quinn ignored them, his gaze locked on Alicia's face, trying to gauge her reaction.

At first, there was confusion. "What?"

"He didn't die in the explosion in Sanselmo," Quinn explained, trying to soften his normal blunt tone as he watched her emotions flicker across her face in a constant, changing stream. Confusion became disbelief, then anger, then consideration, and finally, shining like jewels in her dark, dark eyes, the first radiant gleam of hope.

"They identified his body. We supplied DNA samples—"

"I arranged for the DNA to match the body of the cadaver we planted in the warehouse," Quinn said.

She shook her head. "That was three years ago. If he's still alive—"

"He's still technically a fugitive from the law," Quinn told her quietly. "We weren't ready to bring the truth out into the open."

Confusion returned to her expression, and her voice hardened. "What truth? Why would the CIA help him after all he did?"

"Most of what he did was spy on *El Cambio* for us."

Next came the shock, tempered only slightly by a hint of guilt and dismay. "He was working for the CIA the whole time?"

"Not the whole time. But after the first eight months? Yes. He was."

One grimy hand fluttered up to cover her trembling lips.

"The bomb in the harbor warehouse was meant to be his way out. Nobody was supposed to die except him, you see. The other casualties weren't planned. Cabrera sent some of his men to the warehouse early to make sure your brother wasn't pulling a fast one. Seems he'd begun to suspect Sinclair of not being a loyal soldier for the cause."

"My God," she murmured, dropping her hand away from her mouth. Her dark eyes widened as all the implications of what Quinn was saying apparently began to sink in. "That's why Cabrera took me? To get to Sin?"

"Cabrera never said?" Jake stepped up, putting a comforting arm around Alicia's shoulders.

She looked up at her husband's twin. "He never said. I thought it had something to do with the Coopers' problems with the Cordero drug cartel or something. You know *El Cambio* and the cartels are all knotted up with each other." She looked back at Quinn. "Where's Sin? Why isn't he here?"

It was Jesse Cooper who answered. "He's gone after the woman you barreled over in Cabrera's camp."

She looked at her boss, frowning. "The FBI agent?"

"At the time he left, she hadn't checked in yet."

"But if he's still a fugitive—"

"Seems they knew each other before," Quinn said.

Alicia's gaze wasn't the only one that swung his way at his statement.

"Before when?" Luke asked.

"Before now," he answered. "Actually, from what I'm told, they met shortly before he joined *El Cambio*."

"And nobody thought to mention that before we let him run off in search of her?" Jesse asked.

"Would it have made a difference?" Quinn asked reasonably.

Jesse frowned but didn't reply.

"He's out there in the woods now?" Alicia asked, her voice edged with a combination of fear and anger. "With Cabrera still on the loose and thinking he's a traitor to *El Cambio?*"

"Technically, he *was* a traitor," Quinn said.

She nearly growled at him. "Why the hell aren't we out there helping him instead of standing around waiting for the damned feds? Or don't in-laws count as Coopers around here anymore?"

The Coopers looked at each other uncomfortably, as if they hadn't yet realized that Alicia's connection to the Cooper family made Solano something close to family as well.

Jake was the first one to speak. "Ah, hell. Which way did he go?"

THERE WAS NO way out. And maybe that was for the best, Sinclair thought, since the showdown between him and Alberto Cabrera was long overdue. They could end the blood feud here. Now. Just the two of them. Nobody else caught in the crossfire.

Too much blood had already been shed because of the two of them.

The FN9 he'd taken off one of Cabrera's men still held seventeen rounds. It might not be a match for the AR-15 strapped over Cabrera's shoulder the last time Sinclair had seen him, but it could do some damage before Cabrera's bullets could take him down.

It would be a fitting final act to his own sorry life, he thought, to make sure Cabrera never got the chance to kill another innocent.

He crouched low in his hiding place between two of the tents, keeping his ears open for sounds of Cabrera's movement. So far, the terrorist leader seemed to have no fear, no sense that he might not be alone in the encampment. But Sinclair didn't let himself believe there was a chance to take Cabrera out without risk to his own life. Whatever else he might have been, might still be, Sinclair knew he wasn't the sort of man who could fire on someone who didn't fire on him first. Not without another life at stake.

He'd already searched the whole camp. No sign of Ava. Alicia was safely in the protection of the Coopers. And Cabrera had sent all his men into the woods to look for their missing comrades and their escaped captive.

He and Cabrera were alone.

Time to end it.

But as he settled himself to wait, he realized he no longer heard Cabrera moving around. Frowning, he tamped down the urge to move from his hunkered position to see where Cabrera had gone and listened harder for any sound of movement outside the tents.

When it came, it was loud and impossibly close. The harsh, metallic click of a revolver cocking inches from his ear.

"Oh, this is delicious." Instead of Spanish, Cabrera spoke in perfect, lightly accented English. He'd gone to college in the U.S., Sinclair knew, though by the time they'd met in the jungles of Sanselmo, Cabrera had eschewed English almost completely in favor of his native language. But he'd been quick to tell Sinclair about his time at UC Berkeley, where both of Sinclair's parents were professors. Cabrera had taken classes from both of his parents. Sinclair had never figured out whether Cabrera considered Sinclair's connection to Martin and Lorraine Solano to be a plus or a minus.

"Took you long enough," Sinclair answered in English as well. "I've been waiting for you here a long time."

"You have your sister," Cabrera murmured, his voice laced with suspicion. "So why would you come back here?"

Sinclair wasn't about to tell him about Ava. If she wasn't here, that meant she was still somewhere out there in the woods, possibly attempting to avoid the *El Cambio* search party. He wasn't about to put Cabrera and his men on her scent.

"No answer?" Cabrera prodded.

"Just wanted to catch up with old acquaintances," Sinclair answered, starting to turn toward Cabrera.

The hard edges of Cabrera's gun barrel pressed firmly into the flesh at the side of Sinclair's head. "Put down your weapon. Or," he added after a beat, "perhaps I should say Carlito Escalante's weapon?"

Sinclair lowered the FN9 to the ground. Cabrera kicked it, letting the steel toe of his boot thud solidly into Sinclair's thigh.

Sinclair gritted his teeth against a sharp explosion of pain in his leg.

"Any other weapons?"

He wasn't about to let Cabrera strip him of his Taurus. He'd go down fighting first. The revolver gleaming in his peripheral vision would be easier to deal with than the AR-15 that was no doubt still strapped over Cabrera's shoulder, but it would be lethal enough if he lost his last weapon.

Cabrera jabbed the barrel of the revolver against his head hard enough to send pain skating through his scalp and down the back of his neck. He felt a trickle of wetness sliding down his temple and realized the edge of the gun barrel had drawn blood that time.

"Weapons?"

"You're just going to kill me anyway," Sinclair growled, wondering how quickly he could get the Taurus out of the holster attached to his ankle. Quickly enough that Cabrera couldn't blow a hole in his head as he moved?

Not likely.

"What are you waiting for?" he asked when Cabrera didn't respond. "Why don't you just go ahead and shoot me?"

"You tempt me beyond words," Cabrera said sharply.

"If you really wanted me dead, you'd have shot me. But you don't, do you?" Sinclair moved his head slowly to the side to look up at Cabrera. As he did so, his gaze snagged on a flicker of movement in the wooded slope rising behind the camp. Whatever moved went still before he could identify what he'd seen, but he let his gaze linger a moment longer.

"Oh, I want you dead," Cabrera assured him. "I will kill you today. But first, I must know why."

"Why what?" Sinclair asked, softening his focus on the woods in an attempt to spot any further movement among the trees.

"Why you betrayed me."

Betrayed me, Sinclair silently echoed Cabrera's words. Not *El Cambio.* Not the cause. But Cabrera himself.

He'd known Cabrera's vendetta must be personal. But he hadn't realized just how personal.

"We were comrades. Compadres." Resentment suffused the terrorist's soft words. "I entrusted my plans to you, and you betrayed me."

"You murdered Luis Grijalva. You stood on the most sacred site of Sanselmo history and took him down like a rabid dog."

Cabrera spat out an obscenity in Spanish before he regained his composure. "He was no rabid dog," he resumed in English. "He was a mouse. A gutless, scared little mouse who lacked the machismo to do what the revolution required."

"There was no revolution left." Just as Sinclair had concluded he'd imagined the movement in the woods, he saw another flicker of motion. A head peeking out from behind the trunk of a tree. Tangled brown hair, barely visible above a camouflage-painted face.

Ava. His heart contracted painfully with a jolt of terror.

She was out there, watching. And if there was one thing he'd learned about Ava Trent over the past three days, it was that she had the heart of a lion and the soul of a warrior.

She was out there in the woods right now, intent on finding a way to come to his rescue. He knew it as surely as he knew the sound of his own voice.

And her lion's heart and warrior soul would get her killed if he didn't find a way to stop her.

He struggled not to let his fear show as he turned his gaze to meet Cabrera's, scrambling mentally for the dangling thread of their conversation. "The revolution was over before I ever set foot in Sanselmo," he continued, hoping the trembling in his legs didn't make it to his voice. To his own ears he sounded impossibly calm.

He hoped he wasn't fooling himself.

"That is a lie," Cabrera spat. "The revolution continues, even today."

"You want power and money. You want carte blanche to punish the world for your shortcomings, to hide your animalistic rage behind a cloak of revolutionary zeal. You killed Grijalva because he reminds you of your own failures. Your own lack of machismo."

Cabrera swung the butt of the revolver toward Sinclair's head, his movement impulsive and made jerky by his rage. Sinclair had just enough warning to duck, the hard edge of the gun butt scraping against the side of his head rather than landing a direct blow.

On his hands and knees, he spared a desperate glance toward the woods, hoping Ava would stay put.

Of course, she didn't. She was already on the move, her pistol gripped in her right hand while she used her free hand to balance as she scrambled in a crouch down the shallow slope.

Don't do it, Ava!

He ducked belatedly at a flurry of motion in his peripheral vision. The butt of Cabrera's revolver caught him squarely in the cheek, sending a blinding cascade of sparkling stars across his field of vision as pain exploded through his brain.

The stars twinkled out, but the pain kept pounding a brutal cadence through the side of his face, rolling in syncopated waves of agony.

"I *am* the revolution," Cabrera declared. *"Soy La Curva de la Muerte."*

Ava was getting close now, Sinclair saw as he let his gaze slide her way. Too close. Soon, Cabrera would see her. He would fire on her, and there would be nothing Sinclair could do to stop him.

There was nothing he wouldn't risk to stop that nightmare from happening.

Grabbing Cabrera's arm, he jerked the man around to face him until the terrorist's back was turned to Ava. "You are nothing, Alberto. You are the garbage real men wipe from their shoes."

Cabrera responded by pressing the barrel of the revolver against the center of Sinclair's forehead.

"And you," Cabrera answered in a rush of cold fury, "are a dead man."

Chapter Sixteen

Ava froze in place, shuddering as her sudden stop sent pebbles tumbling down the hill in front of her. Once Sinclair grabbed Cabrera, turning him so that his back was to Ava, she knew Sinclair had spotted her.

But all rational thought fled her brain in a heartbeat when she saw Cabrera press the revolver to Sinclair's head. His voice rose to a crescendo of rage, ringing through the woods.

"And you are a dead man."

No, no, no. She was still too far away, her skill with the unfamiliar MK2 too unpredictable to make the shot.

"Kill me now and you'll never know which of your trusted men is a traitor," Sinclair replied. He sounded unnaturally calm, she thought. As if he didn't fear anything. Not even his own death.

That idea scared her nearly as much as the sight of Cabrera's finger trembling on the trigger.

She made her fear-paralyzed limbs move, took a careful step down the hill. If Sinclair could just stall Cabrera until she was close enough to take a decent shot—

"There is no other traitor," Cabrera declared, harsh laughter tinting his voice. "My men worship me."

"Your men fear and loathe you," Sinclair replied with contempt.

Stop it, Ava thought as she pushed her way downhill more quickly, afraid that Cabrera had already neared his snapping point. *Stop antagonizing him. Stall him, don't push him into pulling the trigger!*

"You think you're brave? You think you show courage speaking to me this way?" Cabrera asked. "You are a fool."

She was close. So close. Just a few more yards...

Her foot slipped on a loose rock, sliding out from under her. She tried to catch herself without falling, but her scramble for footing dislodged more rocks, and there was nothing quiet about their tumbling cascade down the slope. They clacked like castanets against each other as she ended up hitting hard on her backside, the jolt jarring up her spine until her teeth crashed together, making her see stars.

When her sight flooded back a second later, she was staring down the barrel of Alberto Cabrera's revolver.

CABRERA WHIRLED AT the sound of rocks falling behind him, his revolver already whipping up toward Ava. She'd dropped her gun hand to stop her fall, leaving her utterly defenseless.

With no time to go for his own weapon, Sinclair threw himself on Cabrera's back and went for the revolver.

The gun fired with a deafening crack, and Ava cried out.

Sinclair tried raise his head to relocate her position but Cabrera had wrapped his arm around his neck and was pulling him down to the ground with him, grinding his forehead into the dirt. Sinclair tightened his grip on Cabrera's gun arm and locked his legs around the man's thighs to hold him immobile while they struggled for control over the weapon. His fingers dug into Cabrera's chest.

No, he thought. Not his chest—

Cabrera slammed his elbow into Sinclair's chin, knocking his head back with a jarring crash of bone on bone. Sinclair's grip on Cabrera's wrist slipped, and he felt himself falling away, his head spinning from the impact. He grabbed at the man's legs just as Cabrera brought the pistol up again.

A crack of gunfire split the air. But it hadn't come from Cabrera's pistol, Sinclair realized as Cabrera reeled backwards, staggering to keep his footing. Sinclair reached for the Taurus 1911 tucked into his leg holster, his suddenly sluggish brain trying to catch up, to tell him something important.

Something life-or-death.

Cabrera didn't fall. He threw away the pistol and grabbed the AR-15 rifle that had fallen to the ground during his struggle, swinging the rifle barrel toward Ava just as she fired another shot.

The bullet hit Cabrera in the chest. Sinclair saw him take the body blow and reel backward again.

But he still didn't fall.

Vest, he thought. He's wearing a protective vest.

And Ava wasn't.

He could go for a headshot, but if he missed, it would be too late. There was no time to aim.

Once again, he threw himself at Cabrera. The AR-15 barked three times in rapid succession as they tumbled to the ground. Sinclair prayed Ava hadn't been in the line of fire.

Then, suddenly, she was there, flinging herself on top of Cabrera's head and shoulders. She trapped the rifle under one knee and clamped his head between her knees, shoving the barrel of the MK2 against the base of Cabrera's skull.

"Move again," she growled, her breath coming in harsh gasps, "and I will fire two bullets into your brain stem. *¿Comprende?*"

Cabrera went utterly still.

Sinclair wiped a film of blood from his head wound out of his eyes and met Ava's wild-eyed gaze across Cabrera's prone body. "You hit?"

"No," she breathed. "You?"

"Not with a bullet," he answered, poking at the swollen lump on his cheekbone. His jaw didn't feel too great, either.

But he'd live. At least, he would if they could avoid the rest of Cabrera's men.

"His men are out looking for you and the others," he warned.

"I know. I almost ran into one of them." Between her knees, Cabrera hissed something Sinclair couldn't quite make out. But Ava seemed to understand what he said, if the rough jab of her pistol barrel against his neck was anything to go by. "I told you to stay still," she rasped.

Sinclair grabbed the butt of the AR-15 and nodded to Ava. "Move your knee."

She let up pressure on the rifle and he jerked it from Cabrera's grasp. He considered tossing it aside before he remembered they weren't out of danger yet. He slipped the strap over his own shoulder instead.

"Can you grab the phone out of my pocket and contact Jesse?" she suggested, both of her hands still occupied with keeping Cabrera in place.

As Sinclair started to reach for the phone, he saw a half-dozen camouflage-clad figures glide into view, coming at them from what seemed like every direction.

He already had the AR-15 in his hands before the nearest man held up his hand and he recognized the sharp blue eyes of Jesse Cooper.

He let loose a flurry of profanities as his whole body turned into a trembling mass of nerves. "You damned near became a casualty, Cooper."

"That Cabrera?" Jesse asked, nodding at their captive.

"Yes, but his men are still out there."

"Yeah, well, so are the Feds, finally." Alexander Quinn stepped forward, stopping to look down at Cabrera. "You'd have saved us all a lot of time and money if you'd just shot him."

Sinclair glanced at Ava, letting himself drown a little in her mountain-pool eyes. "She did."

"It didn't take," she murmured, her lips curving in the faintest hint of a smile.

"Sin?"

The voice, soft but so familiar it made his chest ache, came from behind him. He closed his eyes against the sudden flourish of pain, almost hoping he'd imagined her voice.

"Oh, my God, Sin."

He opened his eyes and she was there, almost a decade older and even more beautiful than he remembered, despite her ragged appearance, pale face and shadow-smudged eyes. Tears burned like acid in his eyes and he blinked them away, not wanting anything to mar his first look at his sister in over eight years.

"I'm so sorry, Ali," he whispered. The words seemed to scrape his throat raw. "I'm so sorry."

Quinn bent next to him, grabbing Cabrera's legs. He nodded for Sinclair to move away from the captive. "I've got him."

Sinclair rose on unsteady legs, barely able to hold his

sister's wide-eyed gaze. Love and shame battled inside him, two sides of the same emotion, each vying for supremacy.

"Why didn't you let us know?" Alicia asked, tears sliding over her cheeks.

Answering despair roped around his chest and squeezed as he searched for an answer that wouldn't break her heart and his.

"He couldn't," Ava said in a flat tone when he didn't answer. She'd come to stand near him, he saw. J.D. Cooper had taken over restraining Cabrera. "He knew you couldn't keep that secret from your parents."

A hard jolt of pain zigzagged through him at her words. Not because of the implied insult to his parents but because she understood, instinctively, what had kept him silent.

He loved his parents, but he didn't trust them to choose his word over that of people they considered their ideological allies. They'd never seemed to move past their own youth, when radicalism was romantic, exciting and, in some cases, worthwhile.

They'd never apologized for their association with killers, preferring to pretend that the deadly incidents were tangential to the work of the Journeymen for Change and that the widespread destruction of businesses and property their bombs had wrought had been entirely defensible.

Would they choose the side of the son who'd sold his soul to the CIA?

"Of course," Alicia murmured. "You'd been working for the CIA. Martin and Lorraine Solano's son." Her lips curled in a bleak smile. "They'd have been appalled."

"I knew you hated me anyway. I thought maybe it would be best for us all if we just left it that way," he admitted, loathing how cowardly the explanation sounded.

"I never hated you. I was angry and hurt by the things I

thought you'd done, but I could never hate you." She took a step away from her brother-in-law, a step toward Sinclair. "For the record, if you'd told me the truth, I would have kept it from our parents. I'm not blind to the way they are."

"You were so young when I left. I wasn't sure—"

"I never romanticized what our parents did, like you did."

He nodded slowly. "So that just leaves cowardice, I guess. I didn't want you to see what a fool I'd been."

"You weren't a fool." She took another step toward him, moving with care, as if she saw him as a wild animal on the brink of flight. He almost smiled at the thought, because in so many ways, that was exactly who he'd been for the past few years. "You were young and conscientious. Looking for something in this world worth believing in. You just chose the wrong thing. But if anything Quinn's been telling me is true, you paid for that mistake beyond what anyone could have asked of you."

"Don't." His voice came out rough and hard, even though he hadn't intended it. "Don't turn me into a hero."

"Too late for that, bud." Ava slapped his shoulder from behind, making his nerves jangle. "You're already a hero."

He glanced at her, saw the emotion blazing in her hazel eyes, and felt like a fraud. He wanted to yell at her, at Alicia, at all of the Coopers standing there looking at him with admiration and sympathy.

They didn't know. They didn't understand what he'd done.

But he didn't get the chance to respond. The sound of dozens of feet crashing through the woods around them put everyone on alert. The Coopers whipped around to face the newcomers, weapons raised and ready.

"Put down the weapons!" The command filtered through a bullhorn, ringing through the woods.

Dozens of black-clad men and a couple of women circled the encampment, a variety of pistols and rifles aimed their way.

The Feds had finally arrived.

AVA HAD NEVER been the most patient of women, but her years in the FBI had taught her that justice had its own timetable, and it was almost always slower than she liked. Always before, she'd managed to tamp down her irritation with the slow grind of bureaucracy and let the situation play out to its natural end.

But Sinclair Solano was a hero, not a terrorist. And so far, not a single FBI agent, not even her SAC, Pete Chang, would listen to her.

"He's not dead, so the warrant for his arrest stands," Chang told her in a voice that suggested he suspected her of having lost her mind during her days with Sinclair Solano.

"Stop looking at me as if I have Stockholm syndrome," she growled. "I wasn't his captive. He was mine. And if you don't believe me, go find Alexander Quinn and he'll tell you."

"Mr. Quinn seems to be hard to find at the moment," Chang told her with a grimace. "And from what I've heard, he's hardly what you'd call a reliable witness. The man spent two decades lying for a living."

"Then talk to the Coopers."

"Solano's in-laws, you mean?"

If there had been anything in the interview room to wrap her hand around, she'd have thrown it at Chang, her career be damned. "If you put him in prison, he will be at Cabrera's mercy. You think *El Cambio* doesn't have a prison network?"

"I know they do." Chang's placating tone scraped

every nerve she had. "I'm sure the courts will make sure Solano's put in solitary."

"He doesn't belong in jail at all!" Ava gripped the edge of the table in front of her, frustration boiling inside her. "He put his life on the line for this country for five years."

"He blew up nine people in Tesoro."

"Nine terrorists who showed up before they were supposed to. The bomb was meant to go off with no one in the warehouse."

"So your buddy Solano says."

"So Alexander Quinn said."

"Quinn again."

Ava clamped her mouth shut. "I want to see Solano."

"I don't think that's a good idea."

"With all due respect, sir, I don't care what you think about the idea."

Chang's eyes narrowed. "You're treading a very dangerous line, Agent Trent."

"Then let me stomp all over it," she said, her patience gone. She pushed to her feet and glared down at the SAC. "I quit."

Chang's dark eyebrows rose. "I beg your pardon?"

"I no longer work for the Federal Bureau of Investigation, effective immediately." She pulled her credentials wallet from her pocket and shoved it across the table to him, then turned to go.

Chang grabbed her arm, jerking her back to face him. "Nobody said you could leave."

"Are you charging me with anything?"

Chang looked as if he'd like to say yes, but finally he shook his head and let go of her arm. "No."

Only because the fallout would be a PR nightmare, she thought with an inward grimace.

"It was nice working with you, Pete. Well, up to today."

She spared him a final, regretful look, and walked to the interview room door.

It was locked, but when she hammered on the door, the guard outside opened it and didn't try to stop her when she walked into the hall.

A half-dozen of her fellow agents and several Poe Creek police officers watched her with curious expressions as she silently walked the short gauntlet of onlookers toward the front exit of the Poe Creek police station. As she stepped outside, a blustery wind blew needles of rain into her face and she remembered with dismay that her car was back in Johnson City. She and Landry had come to Poe Creek in a bureau-issue sedan.

With a groan of exhaustion, she dropped to the top step of the police station's shallow front stoop and fought the urge to cry.

"Need a ride?"

She looked up to see Hannah Cooper looking down at her with sympathetic eyes. "How'd you know?"

"Tiny police station. Voices carry." She offered her hand to Ava, helping her to her feet.

"Don't suppose you know where they've taken Sinclair, do you?" she asked Hannah as they reached a rental sedan parked near the edge of the visitor's parking area.

"No. Alicia sent me in search of answers, but nobody's talking." Hannah adjusted the steering wheel and buckled her belt before looking across the seat at Ava. "I guess you didn't get any answers, either."

"No. Apparently I'm an unindicted co-conspirator to Sinclair, as far as the FBI is concerned." She found the strength to strap the seat belt around her and slumped against the seat. "He's a terrorism suspect. You know as well as I do he could be halfway to some secret CIA interrogation facility by now."

"The CIA knows who he is and what he really did," Hannah reminded her. "I'd be more worried that someone in Homeland Security wanted to make a name for himself off Sinclair's reputation."

Ava groaned. "Thanks. That makes me feel so much better."

"Quinn's gone back to Purgatory. He said he has better resources back at The Gates and thinks he can at least find out where Sinclair is." Hannah was heading back toward the motel, Ava realized. She supposed the rest of the Coopers had decided to rendezvous there once the FBI finished debriefing them.

"Are any of you in trouble?" she asked.

"Our Alabama concealed-carry licenses are good here in Tennessee, our weapons all comport with state and local laws, and the only shots we took were in self-defense." She shot Ava a weary grin. "Plus, our legal team is formidable enough to give even the FBI nightmares. I think we're good."

"How's Gabe?"

"A lot better now that Alicia's back."

"Did Alicia and Sinclair get any more time together before the Feds took him away?" Ava had been whisked into protective custody so quickly that she'd missed most of what had happened at the camp. During her two-hour debriefing at the police station, she'd managed to learn that the rest of Cabrera's men had been rounded up.

A local doctor had also examined her right there at the station, cleaned and re-bandaged her gunshot wound, given her an antibiotic shot and ordered her with kindly sternness to see her personal physician as soon as possible to get a prescription for more antibiotics.

She'd expected a little more pushback about the four *El Cambio* thugs she, Sinclair and the Coopers had killed, but apparently neither the FBI nor local law enforcement was eager to arrest American citizens for shooting foreign terrorists in self-defense. She might yet have to lawyer up, but for now, she knew better than to ask any questions when they were letting her walk out a free woman.

If only Sinclair had received the same treatment.

"No. They grabbed him up pretty fast."

"And whisked him away to God knows where."

"We're going to find him," Hannah said with quiet fervor as she slowed the car to turn into the motel parking lot.

Ava nodded, but she couldn't quite muster up the same confidence. She knew how Byzantine a system they were dealing with.

By turning in her badge, she'd just locked herself on the outside. And thrown away the key.

Chapter Seventeen

As incarceration on a charge of terrorism went, Sinclair supposed his stay in the federal custody could have been worse. He'd been stuck in the federal prison in McCreary, Kentucky, undergoing intensive interrogation for three days, but nobody had waterboarded him, and any sleep deprivation he was dealing with came from his own copious store of old, familiar regrets.

They had kept him in solitary so far. One hour of physical activity, alone, outside his cell. The other twenty-three hours were spent in his cell, also alone, or across the table from a steady stream of less-than-friendly representatives of a veritable alphabet soup of federal law enforcement agencies.

It came as no surprise when the guard rapped on the bars of his cell around ten on the morning of his fourth day of custody and told him he had another visitor.

The visitor, however, came as a surprise indeed.

"You're looking better than I expected," Jesse Cooper said, his expression neutral but a hint of sympathy warming his blue eyes. "How're they treating you?"

"Like a terrorism suspect." Sinclair took a seat at the table across from the Cooper Security CEO, rattling his shackles to underscore his point. "How'd you talk your way in here?"

"Some people high in the government owe me a favor or two."

"Don't suppose you could call in a chip to get me out of here?"

"I can do better than that. I convinced Gerald Blackledge to give Alexander Quinn twenty minutes of his time."

"Senator Gerald Blackledge?" Sinclair asked. "The same Senator Blackledge who called me vermin in a *60 Minutes* interview?"

Jesse's lips twitched at the corners. "Yes, that Gerald Blackledge."

"God help me."

"That's up to God, but Gerald Blackledge knows a hero when he hears about one. He's all over the Department of Justice to cut you loose and give you a damned medal while they're at it."

Sinclair frowned. "I'm no hero."

Jesse shrugged. "Not sure you're going to convince many people of that when they hear the risks you took in Sanselmo working for the CIA."

"The CIA's never going to let that information go public."

"You're probably right." Jesse folded his hands on the table in front of him, the skin over his knuckles tightening as he leaned forward a few inches and pinned Sinclair with his cool blue gaze. "So let's get to the next part of this interview. Why did you tell the warden you wouldn't see Alicia if she showed up for a visit?"

He hadn't thought she or anyone else he knew would be able to find him this quickly. The Feds had worked hard to keep the news of his arrest from reaching the newspapers until they'd made sure all of the *El Cambio* elements who'd sneaked across the border with Cabrera had been rounded up. But just in case the Coopers were as good as he'd heard—and apparently they were—he'd made sure his sister was on the "do not admit" list.

"I don't want her to see me here," he said.

"She spent years thinking you were a dead terrorist. I doubt seeing you here is going to make her think worse of you."

"She needs to forget she ever saw me again. Go on with her life like it was. She's happy, isn't she? With her work and her marriage?"

"She is." Jesse's eyes narrowed. "She'd be happier if you were part of her life again."

"How'd you find me so fast?"

"Blackledge, again. In some ways, he's more powerful than the president."

Sinclair supposed so. The wily old Alabama senator had been in congress for over two decades, and he had the clout and powerful committee assignments that came with that sort of longevity. "My parents would have a stroke if they knew Blackledge, of all people, had made himself my benefactor."

Jesse Cooper grinned at the comment. "That's what Alicia said."

Sinclair had assumed his sister had informed their parents he was still alive, but if either of them wanted to see him, he hadn't heard any word that they'd tried to make contact. "Do my parents know I'm alive?"

Jesse's grin faded. "Yeah. They're still processing the information."

A kind way of saying they weren't yet decided on whether to forgive him for working with the CIA against a group for which they'd had a lot of sympathy. Of course, they probably still saw *El Cambio* through the rose-colored lenses of their romantic radicalism.

Eight months with *El Cambio* had crushed his own illusions into dust.

"Alicia says to tell you they'll come around. Eventually."

He suspected his sister was overly optimistic. He'd known when he'd taken up Alexander Quinn's offer of an undercover assignment that his parents would probably never understand his choice.

But Martin and Lorraine Solano hadn't stood in the shadows on *La Curva del Muertos* and witnessed Alberto Cabrera slice an old, deluded man damned near in two for daring to question *El Cambio*'s actions and motives.

"Ava Trent resigned from the FBI."

Sinclair's gaze snapped up to meet Jesse's. "Resigned? Or was pushed out?"

"Resigned. Although she seems to think they'd have pushed her out sooner or later, since she wasn't going to toe the Bureau line about you."

"She shouldn't have let me screw up her career," he muttered, swamped with regret.

"She said you'd say that."

"Does she know I'm here?" He hadn't put her on the "do not admit" list, he realized. He supposed he hadn't thought she'd try to find him, considering the hell he'd brought into her life over the past week.

Or, maybe, he'd secretly wanted to leave open the possibility that she'd show up one day, flash those pretty hazel eyes at him and declare her undying devotion?

Fool.

"She does," Jesse said. "She's here, as a matter of fact."

Despite his best efforts, he couldn't quell a rush of excitement. "Here in McCreary?"

"Here, waiting in the warden's office."

A flood of adrenaline jolted through him, doubling his

heart rate in seconds. Ava was here. She was here. If he asked, someone would bring her to see him.

He could almost picture her, those mountain-pool eyes, that wicked smile. Those delicious curves he could still feel under his palms as if his hands had perfect memories.

Jesse's eyes narrowed again. "Are you going to let her see you?"

He clenched his fists around the chains of his shackles. "Not like this."

Jesse gave him a long, considering look. "Blackledge won't stop until you're out of here. You realize that, right? You won't be here forever."

"It doesn't matter," Sinclair answered, refusing to let himself hope. "There's nothing for me out there anyway."

"Quinn wants you to go back to Purgatory and work for him at The Gates."

"Sure he does."

"You think I'd make something like that up?" Jesse flexed his hands. "Alicia made me promise to offer you a job at Cooper Security instead."

Sinclair laughed. "Don't strain yourself complying."

Jesse smiled. "You're not really right for the kind of work we do at Cooper Security, to be honest. From what little Quinn has told me, your skill set is better suited to investigation. Our company is security-oriented. We have only a small corps of investigators and no current openings."

"I'm not getting out of here anytime soon anyway."

"Clearly, you've never met Senator Blackledge."

Two hard raps sounded on the interview room door. It opened a second later, revealing Dunn, the guard who'd brought Sinclair in shackles from his cell. "Time's up."

"You won't see Ava, will you?" Jesse asked as he stood.

Sinclair almost said yes. But he caught himself before

he made the mistake. "No. Tell her to go home and forget about me."

"Yeah. I'll do that." Sarcasm tinted Jesse's reply.

Once Jesse had gone, Dunn escorted Sinclair back to his cell and relieved him of his shackles with another guard looking on.

"Thanks," Sinclair said.

Dunn's gaze whipped up as if suspecting him of being sarcastic. Only after a long, considering moment did his expression clear. He gave a slight nod as he locked the cell door. "Keep your head down."

Sinclair planned on taking that advice to heart. If he wanted to survive life in prison, he had a feeling he'd need to keep as low a profile as possible.

"WHY THE GATES?" Ava asked a few seconds into her slow circuit of Alexander Quinn's corner office. It was a remarkably Spartan space for a man who'd lived such an exotic life for nearly two decades. A plain walnut desk, a built-in book case only a quarter full. No photographs on the desk, only a blotter and a pen holder.

Quinn leaned back in his leather desk chair, his hands steepled over his flat belly. "Adam Brand suggested it. You know Brand from your time with the FBI, don't you?"

"By name and reputation, mostly." She stopped at the window, her attention snared by the striking view of the mist-shrouded Smoky Mountains to the east. "Why'd he suggest The Gates as the name for your agency?"

"Purgatory. The gate thereof." As she turned to look at him, Quinn's lips curved in what passed, for him, as a smile. "It's a bit fanciful for my tastes, but I'll admit it's evocative. A few good men and women, standing in the breach between heaven and hell."

"Think a lot of yourselves, do you?"

His smile broadened a twitch. "Do you want the job or not?"

She turned back to the window, her pulse pounding a nervous cadence in her ears. Decision time. The offer was better than anything else that had come her way in the month since she'd turned in her creds to Pete Chang and resigned from the FBI. The pay was good, the surroundings gorgeous, and Purgatory was actually a shorter drive from her parents' farm in southeastern Kentucky than Johnson City had been.

But if she was serious about putting her feelings for Sinclair Solano behind her, was it really wise to take a job with the man who'd been his CIA handler for five years?

"I want the job," she said.

Quinn nodded as if he'd never had a doubt what her answer would be. "How soon can you start?"

"Tomorrow." The sooner she got her mind off her regrets, the better. Work would give her something else to think about, at least.

And if the mountains cradling the investigation agency's quaint Victorian mansion-turned-office reminded her a little too keenly of her brief reunion with Sinclair Solano, she'd just have to deal.

"Have a seat while I get the paperwork started." He waved at the pair of sturdy leather chairs in front of his desk as he rose and headed for the door.

She did as he asked, though the minute the door clicked shut behind him, she got to her feet again and returned to the window. The sky visible over the mountain peaks was a tumultuous gunmetal-gray, darker clouds scudding across the sky with a threat of rain.

It reminded her of standing in the parking lot of the

Mountain View Motor Lodge in Poe Creek, locking gazes with a dead man.

She closed her eyes as the door opened behind her, not willing to let Quinn see her regrets.

"Oh, sorry, I thought this was Quinn's office—"

She thought for a second that she'd conjured up the deep, smooth timbre of Sinclair Solano's voice. She turned slowly, expecting to find the room empty, the door still closed.

But a pair of dark eyes stared back at her, widening with surprise. Lean features, even more starkly angular than before, softened around the edges as he spoke. "Ava."

"I thought you'd gone back to California. Family reunion." He'd been released from prison over a week ago. The news reports had gone rabid for the story of the terrorist turned CIA double agent, especially when it became clear that there might be a Solano family feud brewing between the new American hero and his parents.

Interest had finally begun to wane when formal statements from the elder Solanos indicated a reconciliation had occurred during a family get-together at the family's Napa Valley vacation home.

"Yeah, well. It got a little frosty among the grapes, so I thought it was time for a change of scenery." His gaze softened as it wandered over her. "You look good. How's your hip?"

"Mostly healed. Looks like there'll be a scar." There was something surreal about hearing the casual tone of her reply when every nerve ending in her body had sparked alive at the sight of him. She felt herself straining helplessly toward him, iron to a magnet.

"What are you doing here?"

"Taking a job."

He stared at her silently, tension building second by second.

"Is something wrong?" she asked finally when he didn't say anything more.

"Quinn hired me this morning. Officially this time." His brow furrowed. "He didn't mention he'd offered you a job, as well."

"Oh." She tried not to feel the sharp arrow of pain that arced through her chest at the wary look in his eyes. "I haven't signed a contract. I can still decline the job."

"Do you want to decline?"

She wasn't sure what he was asking. Or what the brief flare of animation behind his expression meant. "No. I don't. I need a job, and this one seems right up my alley."

"I wouldn't blame you if you'd rather not run into me every day. Considering what helping me out did to your previous career."

Did he really blame himself for her losing her FBI job? "I quit the FBI. They didn't fire me."

"After what you did for me, you didn't have any hope of advancement."

Probably not, considering how annoyed the U.S. Attorney General had seemed about having a senator turn the prospect of a high-profile terrorism conviction into a forced *mea culpa* for arresting an America hero. But Ava didn't care. It was worth everything she'd given up to give Sinclair a chance at living a halfway normal life again.

Even if he didn't want to live it with her.

"I don't think my prospects were all that good anyway." She wished she could read his mind, see what he was thinking behind those cautious brown eyes. "Have you gotten to spend any more time with your sister?"

He smiled for the first time, genuine emotion peeking

through his wall of reserve. "Yeah, I have. She's surprisingly forgiving, considering."

"You have time to make things up to her now."

"I wish—" He stopped midsentence, his lips pressing together.

"You wish what?" She wanted to believe the flicker of feeling darkening his eyes was for her. But she'd already spent two weeks of her life trying to see him when he was in the federal prison in McCreary, only to have him refuse her attempts at contact.

How much clearer did he have to make his intentions before she'd stop wishing for things she couldn't have?

"Never mind." She turned back toward the window, the mist softening the mountains coming from her eyes rather than the lowering gray sky.

"I wanted to see you." The admission came out hoarse. Raw.

She blinked, tears spilling over her lower lashes. She brushed them away with her fingertips. "Who was stopping you?"

"I stopped myself. I thought it would be better."

"For whom?"

There was a long silence, so long she was tempted to turn to look at him. She managed to stay still, to keep looking at the mountains. No more tears fell. She wouldn't let them.

"For you." His voice was closer when he finally spoke. Inches away, not feet.

She closed her eyes, wondering how close she would find him if she turned around. Once again, she willed herself to remain still. She'd made her intentions clear during her two-week vigil at the prison. If he regretted turning her away, if he wanted to change his decision, he had to do the work.

She was done.

"I didn't have that right, did I?" His voice softened until it felt like a caress. "You have a right to make your own choice. It's not like my track record of decisions is anything to emulate."

"I liked the decision you made to take a stand against *El Cambio,*" she admitted. "Would have been nice to know about it a lot sooner, but you can't have everything."

"The danger for me isn't over. Probably won't be as long as *El Cambio* exists. They took a hit losing Cabrera and his men, but there are others like him. There will always be others like him."

"I know. I knew that when I hung around the prison for two weeks hoping you'd be brave enough to talk to me."

"I'm sorry."

"Are you?" She almost gripped the window sill in order to keep from turning to look at him. "You didn't come here looking for me. If you hadn't walked in to find me here, would you be saying any of this?"

"Not this soon, I guess." He touched her, a light brush of fingertips along the curve of her shoulder. It felt like fire, even through her clothing. She tried not to tremble, but her control over her body went only so far.

His hand closed over her shoulder, the grip almost tight enough to hurt. His voice came out in a raspy half whisper. "I missed you. I thought I wouldn't, not after a few days. I went so many years without seeing you that I'd almost convinced myself I forgot you. But I never did." His breath burned against her cheek as he bent to speak in her ear. "I never will. This is probably a terrible idea, and I should probably tell you to run away from me as fast and as far as you can, but I just can't do it anymore. I don't want you to go. I want you with me. I missed you so much when I was at McCreary that I thought I'd shatter."

A shudder of raw need snaked through her, and her resolve crumbled. Whirling to face him, she wrapped her arms around his waist and pressed her face into the curve of his neck, basking in his heat and his strength as he crushed her closer to him. "I missed you, too."

He kissed her temple, her forehead, and finally her lips. What started as a tender caress caught fire and blazed to an inferno that left her gasping for breath and trembling on the verge of complete surrender.

He tore his mouth from hers, cradling her face between his palms. "This is crazy, isn't it?"

She nodded. "Probably."

His lips curved. "I find I don't care."

She grinned back at him. "I find I don't, either."

He kissed her again. She felt his body vibrating with the strain of maintaining control. She wished she had half his self-control, because her helpless response to his touch was embarrassing.

"Did Quinn mention anything about the company policy toward office relationships?" he murmured against her mouth.

She struggled to think. Had Quinn even mentioned any rules? Hell, right now, she wasn't sure she even remembered who Quinn was. That was how completely rattled she was by Sinclair's kisses. "I don't know."

"Doesn't matter. I can quit if he gives us any trouble." Sinclair kissed her again, tugging her closer.

"My only relationship policy is, don't bring your dirty laundry to work, no sex on company furniture and don't let it affect your work." Quinn's voice sent a quiver of shock through Ava's already rattled nerves.

She jerked away from Sinclair and looked at the man standing in the doorway, one shoulder leaning against the door frame. He held a few sheets of paper stapled together in one hand.

Pushing away from the door, he crossed to his desk and set the papers in front of the chair she'd vacated earlier. "Your contract, Ms. Trent. If you still intend to sign it." Without another word, he left the office, closing the door behind him.

"Do you intend to sign it?" Sinclair reached for her again, brushing a lock of hair away from her cheek.

She looked at the papers on the desk, then back at him. "No sex on the company furniture?"

A slow smile curved Sinclair's beautiful lips. "Does the floor count as furniture?"

She smiled at him, her heart galloping like a thoroughbred in her chest. Brushing her lips against his as she eased herself from his grasp, she crossed to the desk and picked up the papers. Plucking a pen from the holder on Quinn's desk, she slanted a look at Sinclair over her shoulder. "Eight years ago, about three hours into our acquaintance, I called my mother and told her I thought I'd met the man I was going to love for the rest of my life."

His dark eyes shined back at her, full of emotion that only underscored the growing certainty that she was making the right decision, not just about the job but the rest of her life. "What did she say to that?"

"She said I should take my time before I jumped into anything." She clicked the button of the pen and signed the papers, happiness bubbling up in her chest until it erupted in a helpless smile. "I think eight years is enough time, don't you?"

He crossed the space between them and tugged her into his arms, pressing his forehead to hers. "I do," he agreed, his mouth brushing hers. "I really do."

* * * * *

Award-winning author Paula Graves's new miniseries, THE GATES, *is just getting started.*
Look for CRYBABY FALLS, on sale next month, wherever Harlequin Intrigue books are sold!

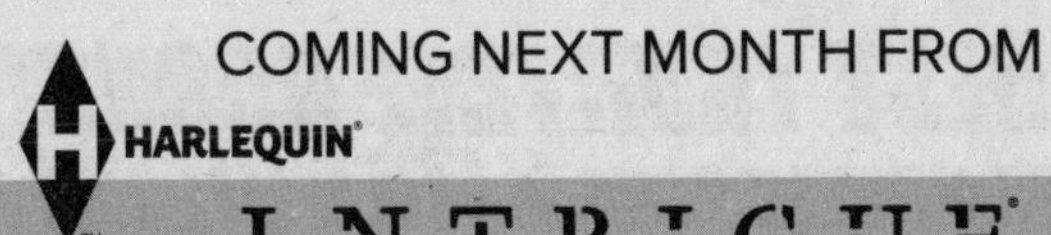

Available September 16, 2014

#1521 COWBOY BEHIND THE BADGE
Sweetwater Ranch • by Delores Fossen
When Ranger Tucker McKinnon finds former love Laine Braddock hiding with newborn twins, Tucker puts both Laine and the babies in his protective custody. Can they keep the newborns safe—and repair their relationship—with a killer closing in?

#1522 CRYBABY FALLS
The Gates • by Paula Graves
A cold case murder brings together PI Cain Dennison and former cop Sara Lindsey. They stumble across information someone wants to keep buried—and a killer who is willing to bury *them* along with it!

#1523 THE HILL
Brody Law • by Carol Ericson
When PI Judd Brody agreed to safeguard socialite London Breck, he expected a fluff gig. But London is nothing like the wild princess he'd seen in the media...and his attraction to her is as real as the threat to her life....

#1524 SCENE OF THE CRIME: BATON ROUGE
by Carla Cassidy
Alexander Harkins is appointed head of a task force to find missing people, and is paired with Georgina Beaumont—his ex-wife. Now the race is on to not only find the victims, but also the reason Georgina left him....

#1525 CHRISTMAS AT THUNDER HORSE RANCH
by Elle James
Border Protection pilot Dante Thunder Horse teams up with a gorgeous paleontologist to uncover the madman attempting to destroy the Thunder Horse lineage.

#1526 TRAPPED
The Men from Crow Hollow • by Beverly Long
Elle Vollman and Dr. Brody Donovan survive a plane crash in the Amazon jungle only to encounter a more dangerous threat. Can Brody save the woman who left him thirteen years earlier?

When a woman from his past shows up with newborn twins and claims she needs his protection, a Texas lawman will risk everything to keep them all safe…

Read on for an excerpt from
COWBOY BEHIND THE BADGE
by USA TODAY *bestselling author*
Delores Fossen

Laine didn't push him away. A big surprise. But she did look up at him. "Ironic, huh? When you woke up yesterday morning, I'll bet you never thought we'd be voluntarily touching each other."

Tucker shook his head, hoping it'd clear it. It didn't work. Maybe he should try hitting it against the wall. "Who says this is voluntary?"

A short burst of air left her mouth. Almost a laugh. Then that troubled look returned to her eyes. "It's not a good idea for us to be here alone."

"No. It's not."

There. They were in complete agreement. Still, neither of them moved a muscle. Well, he moved some. His grip tightened on her a little, and those kissing dreams returned with a vengeance.

"Besides, I'm no longer your type," she added, as if that would help.

It didn't.

However, it did cause him to temporarily scowl. "How

HIEXP69788R

would you know my type?"

Another huff. Soft and silky, though, not rough like his. Her breath brushed against his mouth almost like a kiss. Almost. "Everyone in town knows. Blonde, busty and not looking for a commitment."

He was sure his scowl wasn't so brief that time, but the problem was he couldn't argue with her about it. Besides, the reminder accomplished what Laine had likely intended.

Tucker stepped back from her.

He figured that she'd say something smart-mouthed to keep things light, but she didn't. For a moment Laine actually looked a little disappointed that their little hugging session had ended, and that was all the more reason for him to not pick it up again.

Ever.

Even if parts of him were suggesting just that.

With killers hot on their trail and innocent babies in need of protection, a sizzling attraction should be the last thing on Tucker's and Laine's minds.

Find out how long they'll be able to contain it when the second book in USA TODAY *bestselling author Delores Fossen's* ***SWEETWATER RANCH*** *miniseries, COWBOY BEHIND THE BADGE, goes on sale in October 2014!*

HIEXP69788R